Border
Crossing

Border Crossing

A novel by

Maria Colleen Cruz

PIÑATA
BOOKS

Arte Público Press
Houston, Texas

Border Crossing is made possible through grants from the City of Houston through the Houston Arts Alliance.

Recovering the past, creating the future

Arte Público Press
University of Houston
4902 Gulf Fwy, Bldg 19, Rm 100
Houston, Texas 77204-2004

Cover design by Tina Encarnación

Cruz, Maria Colleen.
   Border Crossing: a novel by Maria Colleen Cruz.
      p. cm.
   Summary: Twelve-year-old Cesi knows all about her mother's Cherokee and Irish family but little about her father's Mexican heritage, and when she finds no answers at home in California, she sets out alone for Tijuana.
   ISBN 978-1-55885-405-5
    [1. Identity—Fiction. 2. Racially mixed people—Fiction. 3. Mexican Americans—Fiction. 4. Family life—Fiction. 5. Voyages and travels—Fiction. 6. Tijuana (Baja California, Mexico)—Fiction. 7. Mexico—Fiction.] I. Title.

                                                     CIP

June 2014
Lightning Source, LaVergne, TN
12 11 10 9 8 7 6 5 4

"Open your face up and sing."

ani difranco

For Mom, Dad and Mike—you gave me the voice to write this book.
For Nadine—you made me finish it.

Chapter 1

I crumpled a twenty-dollar bill and crammed it into the front pocket of my jean shorts. The rest of my money was spread over other places on my body. Twenty-five dollars in my left shoe. Seventeen dollars in my right sock. Forty dollars in my eyeglass case. I read somewhere that when you're traveling, it's good to spread your money out, just in case you get mugged or something.

I really hadn't traveled alone much before. I mean, I went to school and the store and stuff, but I'd never been on a long car or train ride without my parents. That was about to change. I was going on a trip by myself. Not that my parents knew. They thought I was staying at Kathi's house for the weekend. They would never let me go to Mexico all by myself. Even with them I had only been there once, and I was just a baby then. I didn't remember it at all.

I double-checked my Jansport bag. I had a couple of pairs of clean underwear, a brush, two kinda clean T-shirts, my journal, a few Bics, a pack of Wrigley's and a baggie of homemade beef jerky. I was going to Mexico.

I checked my reflection in the hallway mirror. My dark brown eyes slanted at the sides. I looked depressed unless I smiled. I had to remember to smile. Otherwise people would think I was a runaway. They would send me back. But I was not a runaway. I preferred a "run-to." I was running *to* something. I really liked my home. I just thought I would understand it more if I found out some things.

I double-checked my zipper and slipped my sunglasses on. I walked into the living room without making a noise. Even though they thought I was going to Kathi's, I didn't want them to get a chance to look in my eyes. Mom always knew when I was up to something. It's like she's a mind reader. One time when I was four, Mom was in the kitchen defrosting the refrigerator. I was in the living room. I was supposed to be giving my dog, Midnight, three biscuits for good behavior. Instead, I was sharing with him. One biscuit for me. One biscuit for him. One biscuit for me. One biscuit for him. From out of the kitchen, without even poking her head out of the door, Mom called, "Cesi, stop eating all of Midnight's biscuits. You'll ruin your dinner." Very creepy.

Dad wouldn't notice I was going to Mexico if I was wearing a sombrero, eating a burrito and sporting a huge bumper sticker on my forehead that said, "Mexico or Bust!" He was like that. I loved him, but he could be a little dense sometimes.

At the front door I reached for the latch on the screen door. From somewhere in the cool summer darkness that our house took on in July, Mom called, "Cesi? Cesi? Are you leaving?"

"Yeah, Mom," I yelled back, not turning from the door.

"There's a paper bag on the kitchen counter full of avocados. Can you take a few to Kathi's mom?"

I sighed and went back to the kitchen. Our avocado tree had flourished that year and we had avocados coming out of our armpits. We ate avocados at every meal. Anytime we went to visit anyone we gave them avocados. It was getting embarrassing. And I certainly didn't want to lug them to Mexico, but Mom would suspect if I didn't grab some.

I dug into the bag to find the three smallest ones. I figured I was probably going to end up bringing them all the way across the border. I hated to throw away food. Just as I had zipped up my bag for the last time, Mom walked into the kitchen rubbing her eyes. She had pillow creases across her cheeks from napping and her hair was all messed up. "You got some? Maybe you guys can make some guacamole for a late night snack." She ruffled my hair and gave me a sleepy smile.

My heart pounded. I was sure she knew what I was up to. Maybe it was because she had just woken up, or maybe it was the sunglasses guarding my eyes, or maybe her mind-reading switch hadn't been flicked on yet, but she just gave me a kiss and then turned to rummage through the refrigerator for supper. "Have fun, Cesi, but try to get some sleep this time. Last time you were a grouch all weekend."

"I'll try," I said as I returned to the screen door. I took a deep breath and then pushed it open with my toe. The sunlight was bright, even behind my sunglasses. I stepped onto the yellow grass and around the doggie surprise Ebony had left for me. Our grass was always yellow now. The city wanted us to only water once a week because of the drought. California always seemed to be in a drought. The little watering we did only seemed to encourage the weeds and kill the grass.

I stepped onto the cracked sidewalk and looked back at my house. The paint was peeling, the grass was yellow and some of the screens were missing, but I loved it anyway. It was mine. I felt like I would love it even more once I figured out who I was. Who were those people in that house? I just knew I would find the answers in Mexico.

Chapter 2

I wanted to spend some quality time thinking about who I was. I figured, all these grown-ups go around on these big, long searches trying to figure out who they are, and since I have a little time this summer, I might as well get right to it. I mean, if I figure it out now, look how much time I'll be saving when I'm a grown-up. I won't have to take yoga or read books from the "Self-Help" section in the library when I'm my parents' age.

Of course, after I came to this great decision, what I couldn't figure out was—where was I going to start? What was I looking for exactly? I mean, I knew certain facts about myself. The kinds of things anyone would know:

I'm twelve going on thirteen.

I'm four-feet-and-nine inches tall.

My favorite color is purple.

I love my dog Ebony more than any other living thing.

I've got a big brother named Max, who thinks he's all cool because he's in high school and on the football team.

I have bangs, and when they get too long they kinda stick out on the sides, like horns. Mom says that's why my brother calls me *el diablo* (the devil). Max says that's not why.

I have pale, pale skin and my brother has dark, dark skin.

I have a mom and a dad. They're still married. All my friends' parents are.

Everyone calls me Cesi. You pronounce the "C" like an "S" and it rhymes with Jessie. My full name is Cecilia Maryann Álvarez.

My name was a good place to start. I was named after both of my grandmothers. One of my names is Spanish, one English. It makes sense, since one of my grandmas speaks English and one speaks Spanish.

Grandma Maryann was not your ordinary gray-haired, wrinkle-faced, bread-baking grandmother. She always had an unfiltered Marlboro cigarette hanging from her mouth, cowboy boots on her feet, and she drove around in a little red sports car with bucket seats. I loved when she spent the night at our house. I would wake up in the morning to the smell of bacon and coffee and cigarette smoke and the sound of Mom and Grandma chatting away in the kitchen. I loved the way my grandma's hair was short and blonde except for the white streak down the middle. She called it the "Bryant

Skunk Stripe." "You'll get it too, Cesi," she said every time she tousled my hair.

I loved everything about her, except her smoking. I didn't like the way it made her cough every morning when she woke up. She coughed so hard, and for so long, and so loud, that I couldn't even drown it out by pulling the comforter over my head. Max said her cough sounded like it was going to suck her boots straight through her toes and right out of her mouth. I agreed.

Then there's the other grandmother. She's my dad's mom. She's also not your typical grandmother, but not in ways that I liked. First of all, we had to call her Nana; it sounded like I was saying "la la" in a song. I hated calling her that. My best friend, Tracey, called her grandmother Nana too, but like in "banana." Other friends called theirs: granny, grandma, and nanny. All of those were fine, but "Nana" always embarrassed me. It's just too weird to call your grandmother that name. None of my friends had to call their grandmother that.

Then there was the fact that she was old. Yes, I know all grandmas are old, but Nana was *really* old. She walked behind a big metal walker and wore old brown orthopedic shoes. She wore flowery dresses and smelled like Ben-Gay and burnt tortillas. And she wouldn't speak English even though she understood it. So I spoke to her only in English. She answered me only in Spanish. I didn't understand Spanish. Nana knew I didn't understand, but she did it anyway.

My dad tried to teach me some Spanish phrases that I could try out with her. I didn't like to speak Spanish. It embarrassed me. None of my friends spoke Spanish. Only those Mexican girls with their tight braids and cold burrito lunches spoke Spanish. I was certainly not one of them.

Both of my grandmothers lived far away. No grandfathers. My grandmothers seemed to like living all by themselves. Some of my friends' grandmothers lived in "Homes," which they said are kind of like hospitals for old people. I didn't think my Grandma Maryann or Nana would ever live in a home. I couldn't say for sure, but I knew they liked to live by themselves.

I loved going to Grandma Maryann's apartment. She had a green glass jug, which was as big as I was when I sat down. It was filled with pennies and dimes and nickels. Whenever my brother Max and I went to visit, she would let us tip the jug over and keep whatever came out.

In her bedroom she had a big four-poster bed with a fluffy pink comforter and an air conditioner in the window. There was thick tan carpeting that changed colors when you ran your fingers across it. The walls were covered in rose-patterned wallpaper. There was even a lamp in the shape of a rose. Everything about her room was soft and clean and smelled like Grandma Maryann. It's the best room in the world to take a nap. When I was little, I used to pretend I was a princess and this was my bedroom.

Grandma Maryann also had lots of pictures of our family from a long time ago. Each one told a story. There was a picture of me crying on Santa's lap. My brother had a big fake smile on his face, as if he were trying to ignore the fact that his little sister was balling her eyes out. There was a picture of Mom and Dad sitting on the hood of a car. Mom was wearing a blue sundress and Dad was wearing jeans and a T-shirt. They looked so young and clean and new. I always wondered if the teenagers in that picture ever imagined that they would get married someday and have kids. Then there was the picture of my great-grandfather standing in front of his old farmhouse with a fishing pole. Fishing had been his favorite thing in the world to do, and I guess on the day that picture was taken, he had caught a particularly large trout.

Everything in grandma's apartment told a story, not just the pictures. She had Navajo rugs and turquoise bracelets and rings and soft moccasins, all from when she worked with the Navajo on a reservation in New Mexico. She had beautiful terra cotta planters overflowing with all kinds of prickly cacti. Everything in her house had a special place and order. Everything was either tan or beige or green. Everything made sense.

Then there was Nana's house. You could tell it was different even before you got out of the car. It was red. The whole house was painted red. She painted the sidewalk red, too! Her yard was filled with tree-sized rose bushes and her front porch was crammed with green plants, most of them still sitting in the holiday tin foil wrappers she got them in. Pink Easter foiled ferns sat right next to red, white and blue wrapped spider plants.

The first thing I heard (it's the first thing I always heard) at her front door the last time we visited was the Spanish soap operas, *novelas*, blaring in the background. All these people shouted at each other in Spanish. Then somehow, over all the shouting, I heard birds chirping and squeaking and singing. Next thing I knew, my face was buried in Nana's flowered chest and one of her plastic necklaces was digging into my cheek. Then her wrinkly hands pushed me back by the shoulders. She grabbed my cheeks in her claws and cried out, "*¡Ay, qué chula!*"

I answered, "Hi, Nana," and managed to squeeze by and grab a place on the old red velvet couch. I plopped myself down in a cloud of dust and looked around. There were clay figurines everywhere. There was a blue burro carrying a big green sack. There was a little girl in a yellow dress and bonnet with freckles being chased by her brown dog. There was a clown with a round red nose. Then there were the photographs. Everywhere. Tucked into mirrors, stuffed into picture frames, everywhere. Frames covered every inch of space.

Chapter 3

I really didn't feel great lying to Mom about where I was going, but I knew that if I said, "Mom, I'm going to Tijuana, Mexico, all by myself to discover who I really am," she would have said no.

As a matter of fact, she probably would have said, "Cesi, are you feeling all right? Maybe you ate one too many avocados."

I walked through my neighborhood to the Amtrak station. The railroad tracks divided our town in half. I lived literally on the wrong side of the tracks. It was not really a bad neighborhood. I wasn't afraid to walk around alone or anything. But there were a lot of houses that could use a new paint job, or a new car, or a nicer lawn, including ours. The houses on the other side of the tracks had fresh paint, cars for everyone sixteen and over, beautiful green lawns (despite the drought) and big, blue swimming pools. We went to the public pool. It cost fifty cents to get in, and it had two high dives and very cute lifeguards. I took swimming lessons there one summer.

I walked past the park with the pool and watched kids swinging on the tire swing and playing basketball. I wondered why they didn't seem worried at all about the secrets that made them who they were? Didn't they want to know about the people that came before them? Maybe they already did.

I stopped in the park for a drink of water from the fountain. The water was icy cold, but it had the same flavor as the water that came out of our front yard hose. It was a flavor that was almost a spice when the water was cold, but when it was warm, yuck! I knew it would probably be my last drink of public water until I got back from Mexico. If I learned anything about Mexico from watching television, it was, "Don't drink the water." That was okay with me. I liked soda better.

I walked out of the park and up Euclid Street, the street with a lot of car dealerships. Fords, Hondas, Saturns; all shiny and new in the bright July sun. The salesmen did not look so good. They stood leaning on the cars in their dark suits, their bald heads shining with sweat. The balloons and banners hanging around the lot drooped like the men they were trying to help.

As I walked by, I looked to see if there were any sales*women*. Didn't look like it. I wondered why that was. Maybe it was because no women wanted to sell cars or maybe no one wanted to buy from them. Then I wondered how a person decides to be a car salesman.

I've never heard a kid say, "You know what I really want to do when I grow up? Sell Chevy trucks. That would be the best!"

I wondered about stuff like that a lot, how people ended up the way they were. Was it a choice, or did it just happen? These types of questions moved my feet toward the Amtrak station. I realized, as I passed the last car dealership and the last sweating salesman, that maybe they should come with me. Maybe they wouldn't look so unhappy if they knew the answers, too.

Chapter 4

The photographs interested me the most. They're what started me on my little Mexican vacation. You see, Nana had photographs everywhere. Photographs tucked into photographs, sticking out of mirrors, and stuck on the refrigerator . . . just everywhere. But she didn't have any photo albums or any other sense of order. The only place that this disorder didn't touch was her altar.

I found her altar by accident. I had not been feeling well. I had just thrown up. Mom sent me to Nana's bedroom to lie down. You would think their only daughter throwing up would have made them leave, but no. I was stuck in Nana's room, nauseous.

Normally, I liked lying down in other people's bedrooms, especially adults' rooms. Their rooms seemed so safe and clean and grown up. They always smelled older, too, like perfume and shoe leather. They usually had gigantic beds with huge fluffy pillows. For some reason, they were almost always so much darker and cooler than my room.

Nana's room was dark and cool, but that was the only characteristic that her room shared with other adult rooms I knew. Her bed was the same size as mine and it had paper-flat pillows and a yellowed bedspread that she crocheted herself. She was always crocheting something for someone. I had a pair of slippers for every Christmas I'd been alive.

Her room smelled like roses and Ben-Gay and that smell that you sense if you spend a lot of time with old people. And dust. Her room smelled like dust. There was dust everywhere. She had heavy mustard-colored curtains that kept out any sunlight. There was a table where she kept lots of little perfume bottles and a mirror with even more pictures crammed around the edges, and a Bible written in Spanish.

None of this surprised me. It looked like the rest of her house, only smaller. I lay down on the bed and turned over to one side. As I started to close my eyes, I saw something in the corner. On a little plastic table with a lace doily, there was a statue of a black man dressed up like the Pope or someone like him. I knew enough from church to know that he was a saint, but I didn't know his name, or what he was doing in Nana's bedroom on a plastic table surrounded by candles with a rosary lying at his feet.

He was not only surrounded by candles. Four picture frames surrounded him with very ancient-looking pictures in them. Next to them were tiny vases with red hibiscus flowers from Nana's front yard.

I looked closer and noticed that they also each had something next to them. The oldest picture was of a young woman in a very old-fashioned dress. There was a folded fan leaning against the frame. Next to the picture of the lady was a very old picture of a man who himself wasn't very old at all. There was a gold ring next to him. There was a picture of a small girl with very dark skin carrying some flowers, frowning. Next to her picture was a piece of dirty material that looked like it may have been a hair ribbon.

The last picture was the one that surprised me the most. The man in the picture looked like Dad in old pictures I have seen, except this man was wearing a very fancy old-fashioned suit and hat and was standing on a hill. He had a big smile on his face, as if he were laughing at the person taking the picture. He was the only one on the plastic table smiling. His skin wasn't as dark as the rest, but I could tell he was tan even though the picture was black and white. Next to his picture was a bottle of beer. I almost laughed when I noticed it. I knew for a fact that Nana never drank beer.

Those pictures were probably the first things in the whole house that had ever interested me. Who were these people and why were they in this special place? How come the rest of the pictures were crowded by lots of other pictures, but these stood alone? Why were there fresh flowers here, as if someone had just picked them today?

I lay back down and thought more about that little table and who those people could be and why they seemed so important. I had some guesses, but . . . and then I noticed something that was *really* different. There was not a speck of dust on the table, the statue, or the pictures. The rest of the house was covered with dust.

Chapter 5

I stood in the ticket line at the train station behind a woman with a stroller. The woman's hair straggled from her ponytail into little curls at her neck and she kept rubbing her eyes. The baby in the stroller napped. I could see a tiny fist hanging over the side of the chair.

There were at least five people in front of me and twice that many behind me. I tried to be patient and not tap my foot. I practiced what I was going to say at the counter when I bought my tickets. *Yes, Ma'am. I'm here to purchase tickets for a journey to Mexico to visit my family. Certainly, Sir, you can help me. You're much too kind. I'm definitely much older than thirteen.*

I looked around the train station. It was different from what I had expected. It had high ceilings and huge murals on the walls. The murals were of orange groves filled with trees dripping with the fruit. Brown-skinned Mexicans with red bandanas wrapped around their heads filled the baskets with oranges.

I knew a lot of Mexican-American people worked on farms. They picked strawberries, oranges, and pumpkins, depending on the season. I had no idea if any of my family had ever worked on a farm. I knew the workers didn't get paid very much, and that they weren't always treated well. Sometimes they got part of their pay in the fruit they picked. I found this out when I was driving with Mom one Saturday and she stopped the car next to a man with dirty clothes who was standing at the side of the road next to crates of strawberries.

"How much?" Mom asked, after rolling down her window.

"*Cinco*," he answered.

Mom handed me a five-dollar bill and I jumped out of the car and handed it to the man. Then I slid the strawberries into the back seat.

I turned as we drove away and noticed that he was leaning against a fence, acting like he had nothing to do with the strawberries. I asked Mom why.

"It's illegal for him to sell them," she answered.

"Then why is he doing it?" I asked.

"Because he gets some of his pay in berries and I'm sure he can't eat them all and could probably use the money," she said.

"Okay, but why did you just buy them from him if it's illegal?"

"Because I would rather give my money to the person who picked the strawberries than to the man who doesn't pay his workers enough to live on." Her jaw clenched as she said it.

"It's not fair that he doesn't get paid enough," I said. I was obsessed about things being fair.

"No, Cesi. It isn't. It never was," she said.

I thought about the man selling the strawberries as I looked at the murals of the men picking the oranges. They had such serious looks on their faces as they reached for the fruit.

"Miss? Did you want a ticket?" a voice asked.

I looked away from the mural. "Uh yeah, round-trip to San Diego, please."

"$15.00," the ticket seller said.

I handed her my crumpled bills. She looked at me sharply as she uncrumpled them and smoothed them on the counter before she gave me my change and ticket.

No one asked if there was an adult traveling with me, so I thought I was home free. I walked out onto the station platform to board the train.

Chapter 6

Somehow I had fallen asleep in Nana's cool, dusty room. I heard voices in English and Spanish arguing in the living room. The television was still on in the background, making it even more difficult for me to eavesdrop.

I heard Nana say something in a strange, high voice. I didn't understand a word of what she said since she said it in Spanish. Sometimes she would talk in English, but only when Mom was not around. I'm not sure why.

I heard my mother's voice, "What did she say? John? What's wrong?"

I sat up in the dark room and tried to imagine what was going on in there.

Dad answered, "She says I'm embarrassed to be Mexican."

"*Sí, es verdad*," Nana agreed. Sometimes she forgot she's not supposed to understand English. I imagined her folding her arms across her flowered dress with a satisfied smile.

"Why would she say something like that?" Mom asked.

Nana replied in rapid Spanish. All I could understand was that she said "no" a lot.

"What?" I could imagine Mom's flustered look.

Dad said, "I'll tell you about it later. Go get Cesi. Max, go give your Nana a kiss good-bye."

I lay back down on the bed. I closed my eyes and tried to look like I had been asleep the whole time. Mom cracked open the door and said, "Come on, Cesi. I know there's no way you could have slept through that. Let's go." She flicked on the light.

I covered my eyes and rubbed them as they got used to the light and focused on her. "Mom, who are these people over on the table? Do you know what this is?"

I must have looked concerned because Mom smiled and said, "That's Nana's little altar. You know, like they have in church? It's a special praying place for her. That statue is St. Martin, her patron saint."

"But, Mom, who are the people? Why is there stuff . . .?"

"Let's get a move on folks. The traffic's gonna be a killer," Dad called from the living room.

"I'm not sure. Why don't you ask Nana the next time we visit? I'm sure she'd love to tell you all about it. Are you feeling any better?" she asked as she walked back out of the room.

I got up and followed her into the living room. I gave Nana a kiss on her wrinkly cheek then endured the strangling hug I got in return. "I love you, Nana," I said dutifully.

"*¡Ay, qué bonita!*" she answered.

There was no way she could answer my questions if she wasn't even going to answer them in English. Judging from the mood Dad was in, I didn't think he would translate.

I realized my stomach felt much calmer as I settled into the back seat with my brother. Maybe if I was lucky we would stop for ice cream.

Chapter 7

I walked down the train aisle and looked for other kids my age traveling alone. I didn't see any. Every kid was either with a family, or was a teenager. Everyone was talking about what they were going to do in San Diego.

"Mommy! Are we going to see Shamu?"

"Dad, do you think the lions mind being in a zoo?"

"Can I pet a dolphin, Nanny? Can I?"

I smiled as I found empty seats. I slid over to the window and listened to the conversations. I loved the silly questions little kids asked the grown-ups. My eyes focused on the train station. The cement building glared in the harsh sunlight. The conductor called, "All aboard!" and the train moved.

Just then a kid ran through the station doors, waving a ticket in one hand and clutching a duffel bag in the other. He yelled, "Wait! Wait!" I watched him run. He was fast.

The train didn't stop, but it didn't speed up. With the help of one of the conductors, the kid grabbed a handrail and leaped into a car. My car.

I looked over the top of the seat in front of me and watched the kid thank the guy who helped him. "Thanks a lot, man. The next train isn't until noon, and I have to be on my way to Tijuana by then. You saved me a lot of hassle."

Tijuana. That's where I was going. Just as I turned back to my window daydreaming, the boy eased into the aisle seat next to me. He was still panting and clutching his ticket. He turned and smiled at me. He had very dark skin and shaggy black hair under his California Angels baseball cap. It was one of the old-fashioned kind. It didn't have a halo. His teeth were white and straight, but I knew he had never worn braces. "Hi, is anyone sitting here?" he asked.

"No," I answered. Not that it mattered, since he had already sat down. I wasn't sure if I should encourage conversation with a stranger, even if he looked only a few years older than I was. I knew that could be dangerous. On the other hand, we were going to the same place, and maybe he could even help me out. Besides, he had a nice smile.

"I can't believe I caught the train. I was so afraid I was gonna miss it. I made my mom run two red lights. Boy, was she mad!" He slid his duffel bag under the seat in front of him and then extended his hand. "Tony."

"Hi, I'm Cesi." I took his hand. He had the slight accent particular to kids whose parents were from Mexico, but the kids were born here. It was perfect English with a slightly richer sound, as if they used their whole mouths, all the letters in the alphabet too. I always liked that sound.

"Where are you headed? You're all by yourself, right?" He craned his head around to look at the other seats.

"Uh, I'm headed to Tijuana. I've got some family business to take care of there." I didn't think it was very smart to say I was on my own, even if he did have a nice accent.

"I'm going there too, to see my aunt. Actually, she lives a little outside of T.J. on a small farm. I haven't seen her in a while . . . so, you know, a little field trip sounded good." He smiled again.

"Sounds familiar," I answered.

"So Cesi, your name is short for Cecilia, right?"

"Yep." I readied myself for the usual question that came from native Spanish speakers.

"So you must be part Mexican, right?" he asked.

"My dad." People always felt it was okay to question someone's ethnicity, even when they hardly knew them. I subtracted two points from Tony.

"I bet a lot of people ask you that, right?" he asked apologetically.

"You can say that." I hoped I didn't sound rude.

"It must get annoying," he said.

"It does."

He smiled at me again, "Sorry if I annoyed you."

I smiled back. He just earned a point back. "It's okay."

"You know what question I find most annoying? 'Tony, do you speak Spanish?'" He shook his head and leaned back in his seat.

"Do you?" I asked.

"Ha. You got me back. *Sí, señorita. ¿Y tú?*"

I shook my head. The only Spanish I knew I picked up from Sesame Street and Mr. Muñoz, my Spanish teacher. I could say "my knee hurts" *Me duele la rodilla.*

"Well, you're going across the border, aren't you? I better give you a crash course, or who knows how you're going to get around. It's the least I can do after asking the second-most-annoying question in the world."

"What's the first?" I asked, relaxing as I added one more point to his score.

"Is anyone sitting here?" he asked.

We laughed together.

Chapter 8

I sat in my room trying to get my thoughts straight in my journal. That worked for me most of the time. Sometimes my thoughts flew around like butterflies with no real direction. While they were fascinating, flying around like that, I couldn't make heads or tails out of them until I pinned them down. Unfortunately, when you pin a butterfly down it dies. My thoughts were a little heartier than that. Besides, my journal involved no objects sharper than my Bic.

I chewed on the cap of my pen and tried to imagine what I was trying to piece together so that it would make sense. I decided to make a list:

Who were the people in those pictures in Nana's bedroom?

Why was she so upset at my father?

Why was my father so upset that he made us leave so suddenly?

Why?

That seemed to be my favorite word lately.

As I jotted these questions down I heard my parents talking in the living room, which wasn't unusual. They liked to talk, and they usually talked in the living room. But I was usually bored with their conversations, which mainly dealt with their jobs or money. Nothing terribly interesting. Then I heard my mom say something about "your mother" to Dad. I closed my journal and slid to the edge of the bed closest to the door. I tried to lie very still so I could hear.

"Well, you know how it is . . ." (Whir–whir). My fan was drowning out my father's voice. I leapt out of my bed and turned it off, practically tripping over the cord. Something told me most spies were more graceful than I was.

"She must have her reasons," my mom answered.

I heard ice rattling in a glass. It had to be my father's. When he got to thinking, he swirled the ice in his glass until someone threatened to take away his beverage. The more the ice rattled, the more thoughtful he became. After a few more shakes of his glass he said, "She thinks because I don't speak much Spanish anymore, I didn't teach the kids Spanish . . . you know."

My mom answered, "Well, John, I always thought it was silly that you didn't teach the kids. It would be so useful. I certainly don't know why you don't speak it more, at the very least to your own mother."

This was getting interesting. I wanted to see my father's face, but I couldn't decide if going into the living room would make them stop talking or not. I thought it would probably be okay because most private conversations were held in their bedroom.

I got up from my bed and coughed. I was going to get a drink of water, and I would have to walk through the living room to get to the kitchen. I coughed again, to warn them just in case they did want to shut up.

I stepped into the living room and Mom looked at me, concerned. "Are you getting a cough now? First the stomach, now this. I hope you're not getting some sort of flu."

"Uh, no I feel fine. I'm just thirsty." Mom touched my wrist as I walked by, but they continued talking.

"You know how hard it was for me when I was a kid . . ." Dad stared into his iced tea. "I didn't want Max or Cesi to go through that."

I tried to get a glass as quietly as possible. I didn't want to miss a word. It's pretty hard to turn on a sink quietly.

"Well if that was all, why did she get so upset? Why did *you* get so upset?" Mom asked.

I stood in the doorway of the kitchen, looking interested, but not too interested. Neither of them looked up. "I guess Ma feels that the kids know more about *your* side of the family. That you and your mom tell them all kinds of stories, but I don't tell them much. That you know more about being Mexican than I do. But I'm not around as much, and I really don't think my family is that interesting."

Mom laughed. "Neither is mine, but Mom is a world-class storyteller and historian. She can make going to the grocery store sound interesting."

"That's true, but your family stories are all about America. Most of mine are about Mexico, and we're not Mexicans, we're Americans. We didn't come here so that we could look back and wish we were there," Dad said.

Mom got off the couch. "I can't say that I agree with you, John. It's important to know where your family came from, who they were."

Chapter 9

I stared through the window at the scenery speeding past. I knew the outside world wasn't moving. It was the train that moved, but since I couldn't actually feel the train move, it was more fun to imagine the scenery moving past me. Maybe someone with a really long photograph was running alongside the train. I guessed it was a better job than selling cars.

Tony had wandered off to find the bathroom after teaching me a few Spanish words, leaving me to my wacky thoughts. I wondered whether to trust him or not. I stared at the brown backyards that whizzed past my window. Even though they were moving so fast, I could see the junk piled up amongst the weeds: old rusty cars, yellowed strollers, and torn up tires.

Tony made me laugh and he seemed real smart, not to mention that he spoke Spanish and seemed to know a lot about Mexico. He could probably help me. Actually, he probably would. But I just didn't want anyone's help. This was *my* trip. I wanted to walk away from this knowing that I had found the answers on my own, the ones no one would give me at home.

"What's the question?" Tony asked as he slid onto his seat.

"Hmm?" I turned from the window.

"You were just saying something about looking for answers so I thought that maybe you had some questions."

I blushed. I couldn't believe I had been talking to myself out loud. "Oh, just thinking about a math test I have coming up."

"Oh, I see. You're lying to me. That's cool. You don't want to tell me. I hardly blame you. You don't even know me." He bent down and started to rummage through his duffel bag.

I felt guilty. I wondered why I had lied. I had nothing to hide. Maybe I did. I turned back to the window and stared at the brown landscape.

"You must really have something on your mind if you're looking at that depressing scene."

I turned to snap at him and noticed he was holding a pen over a notebook, ready for action.

"What's that?" I asked.

"I like to write. Almost as much as I like to talk. Since you don't seem to want to do any talking, I might as well write until we come to the part where we ride near the coast. That's pretty. Let me know if you see anything interesting." He smiled politely and began to scribble away in his book.

I was dying to know what he was writing, if it was about me, if it was about Mexico. A story, a poem, a letter, all were possibilities. I wanted to peek over his shoulder, but after being rude to him, I didn't think that was the best idea. So I turned back to the window and hoped to at least see a dog run by.

Chapter 10

Mom and Nana seemed to think Mexico was something pretty important, but for some reason my father either didn't think so, or had some reason for not talking about it.

It's true that most of what I knew about Mexico I learned from Mom or school. Most of what I knew didn't seem very important. We ate a lot of Mexican food. Actually, I didn't really know that was unusual until I started eating at friends' houses. They usually ate roast beef and their idea of exotic food was tacos made with those hard shells that came out of a box, not the soft corn tortillas fried in oil that Mom made.

I knew stuff about holidays and music, very basic stuff. Even though my teachers said I had Mexican "culture," I really didn't know much about Mexico, the country. I did know that it was about two hours away from my house by car, but I hadn't been there since I was a baby and I certainly didn't remember that.

I figured the best place to start was the library (Mrs. Alva, the librarian, would be so proud). I woke up early on Saturday and surprised Mom by passing up the Saturday morning pancakes. I wanted to go to the library to do a little research. Mom's jaw dropped and then she said, "You must really be sick, Cesi."

I laughed as I ran out the door into the sunlight. The library was only a few blocks away, but I could hardly wait to start. I knew that I would find my answers there. If I knew a little more about Mexico, I thought I could figure out why my father seemed to hate it so much. I could also learn a little more about me.

This was the first time I had been to the library on a Saturday before noon. I loved walking through the automatic sliding doors and into the cool air-conditioned lobby. The smell of libraries always made me happy. They smelled like millions of books. Books everywhere, just sitting there, smelling up the place with their yummy aroma. Whenever I went to the library, I always pictured those cartoons where they show the scent from really good food tempting the little cartoon guy to follow. The smell of books just made me hungry.

That day I wasn't going to be able to just wander through the stacks like I usually did. I had some work to do.

I walked straight to the geography section in the children's room and pulled out a world atlas. It seemed like a good place to start. I flipped pages until I found a map of Mexico.

All the other maps I had seen showed Mexico hanging off the United States like a giant icicle. Now here it was all by itself, like a hat dropped by an elf. At the same time, it had so much ocean around it, as if it were an ice-cream cone licked skinnier and skinnier by the Pacific and Atlantic oceans. Hmm . . . maybe I should have eaten breakfast.

I spent three hours in the library looking up all kinds of interesting facts about Mexico. I wrote them down in my journal, hoping that when I got home, they would tell me something I wasn't figuring out on my own.

Chapter 11

"I see something interesting," I said quietly. We were riding into Mission Viejo. The houses were bright and tidy and looked like they were made out of thick white clay.

"They make 'em like that so they look like adobe, the stuff those missionaries used to build all the missions," Tony said.

I turned to look at Tony and noticed that he hadn't even looked up from his writing. "How did you know that's what I found interesting? How did you know where we were? You aren't even looking."

Tony looked up. His dark eyes were completely calm. "I've ridden this train tons of times. But the first time I rode through I was so tired of staring at poor people's sorry backyards that I almost jumped out of my seat to see a little adobe. It's nice. But not as nice as the ocean."

"Oh." I felt stupid for being excited.

"Don't take it the wrong way. I mean, I really like them too, but I've seen them millions of times. I get the feeling this is your first trip to the homeland."

"Huh?"

"This is your first trip to Mexico, right?" he asked. I gulped. Here was that annoying truth again. Why did I want to lie to a stranger? Why did I care if I did? "I was here a long time ago, but my family took a car." There. That was the truth. But it didn't give out too much information. Now as long as he didn't ask . . .

"How long ago?" He closed his book and turned to face me.

"I don't remember." I tried to smile. "Want some gum?"

"No, thanks. I'll buy all the gum I'll need from the kids when I get across the border." He smiled and then went back to his writing.

I stared at him, trying to see into his brain. Kids selling gum. That was interesting. I was dying to ask him what he was talking about, but if I did, he would know that I didn't know what I was doing and I didn't want that to happen. Somehow, though, I was beginning to think that Tony might already know that.

Chapter 12

I threw myself onto my bed, dragging my backpack with me. I could hardly wait to crack open the books I checked out and read the notes I had written in my journal. Mom yelled from the kitchen, "Cesi? Is that you?" I could hear her voice coming closer to my room.

I had time to sit up on the bed before her soft knock came at my door. "Can I come in?"

"Sure," I said as I edged myself to the foot of the bed. My Mexico would have to wait a few minutes.

Mom pushed the door open. With one hand she was holding a yellow dishtowel, which she was using to wipe the sweat off her face from cooking in a hot summer kitchen. "How was the library?"

"Fine," I answered.

"So what are you studying now? Are you done with Loch Ness?" She walked to the bed, and I knew she wanted to talk about something more serious. Uh-oh. A walk to the bed is never a simple, 'How's it going?' talk.

"Nah, I got bored with Loch Ness. I think it's all lies anyway. I'm just looking around for a new topic." I loved to study new things. For a while I was into Camelot and the Knights of the Round Table. Then I studied mermaids. The last thing was Loch Ness. I was grateful that Mom was used to me loving the library. It sent her off my trail.

She plopped onto the bed next to me, and put one soft palm to my forehead to brush the hair behind my ear. "Did you hear Dad and I talking the other night when you were wandering around the house?"

I had to think for a minute. I could lie and make her believe I was stupid or I could tell the truth and give myself away. Before my head decided, my mouth was open. "A little. Something about Dad being Mexican."

Mom smiled awkwardly. "You're Mexican too."

"I know," I said.

"You don't wonder about anything? You don't want to know at all what we were talking about?" she asked.

I looked at her. She wanted to be helpful. She thought my questions would be easy ones. I swallowed and decided to ask what I wanted to know anyway. "Mom, why does Nana think Dad's ashamed of being Mexican?"

Mom's eyes opened wide and her mouth tightened, but her voice was steady. She put her hand on my leg and said, "Well, Dad's not the only one she feels that way about. Your aunts are like him, too. Nana just doesn't think he acts very Mexican."

"Like not speaking Spanish?" I asked, sitting up straighter. I might be getting some information.

"Yeah, language is part of it, and other stuff. Like the fact that he married someone who's not Mexican." She smiled when she said that.

"So why's he like that anyway?" I moved so that I could look right at her face.

Mom put both her hands back into her lap and pulled a loose thread hanging off the dishtowel. "That is complicated, Ces. I don't even know if we can say he's not acting like a Mexican. I mean, what's a Mexican supposed to act like?"

"You know what I mean, Mom." I hated when she got all vague like that.

She stood up. "Oh, Cesi. Your Dad lived a really difficult life. He had a hard time growing up, and I think he just wanted to try living the way he lives now. Which I don't think has much to do with whether he's a Mexican or not. Do you understand?"

I nodded because that's what she wanted me to do. But I didn't really understand. I only knew that there must be a deeper reason Dad was the way he was.

Chapter 13

"San Diego!" hollered the train conductor as he briskly walked down the Amtrak's aisles. I pulled myself away from the window. The views had become better as we got closer to the shore. I saw the gorgeous long beaches with surfers bobbing in the waves and families having picnics on the sand. I gathered my stuff and straightened my shirt, feeling around to make sure my money was still all there.

My stomach tightened as I realized that I was about to leave the safety of the train and enter another country. Another country. Weird.

"Hey, wanna walk with me to the trolley? We're both headed the same way; we might as well travel together." Tony flashed his bright smile.

Once again I wasn't sure. I was really starting to like this Tony guy . . . but he was still a stranger. Maybe he was some kind of bait for a crazy kidnapper. . . . But when I looked at his grinning eyes and the hair that kept falling there, I heard myself say, "Yeah, sure."

We climbed off the air-conditioned train, out into

the heat of a San Diego summer. I was already glad I had packed light. It was hot enough without having to lug a big duffel bag along with me.

"The trolley is over this way. It's only a couple of bucks." I climbed on after Tony and settled back to watch the scenery of Downtown San Diego pass slowly by. There were a lot more palm trees out here than there were at home. Would there be many in Mexico?

"Are you really sure you don't want to stop by my aunt's for a little while before you do whatever it is you have to do? It's a free meal—and she's a great cook," Tony offered once again as we got ready to jump off the trolley.

I was about to answer him in a very irritated tone. He wouldn't take no for an answer. But then I thought it would be a great way to save money and see a little more of "the homeland." As my tennis shoes hit the asphalt after Tony's, I heard myself say, "Why not?" I didn't seem to have any control over my mouth anymore.

Chapter 14

I didn't even wait for Mom to close the door before I went back to my book bag. I thought for a brief moment that Mom was going to tell me something important about my father. About me. She even said I was Mexican. But I had no idea what that was supposed to mean.

So Dad's life was hard. Isn't everyone's? I didn't see why that was such a big deal. I cracked open the first book I grabbed from my bag. It was a picture book about traditional dancing in Mexico. The language was very easy, but that's not what attracted my attention. It was the pictures.

The pictures of the dancers were beautiful, especially the pretty girls in their crisp white blouses and brightly colored skirts. Their black hair was pulled into elaborate braids with red ribbons strung through each one. They held their skirts up at their hips and swished them. There were pictures of girls spinning with rainbow circles of color surrounding them. Their black shoes were covered in brown dust, but their skirts and blouses were spotless.

Their deep black hair complimented their brown skin. Each girl was a different shade of brown. Some lighter, some darker. Some looked like Dad. I looked up from the book and into the mirror that hung over my dresser. My skin was a pale shade of pink. Sometimes I felt that if my skin were darker, my hair browner, then I would be more Mexican. Maybe if I could dance like that—twirl my skirts and spin—I would look more Mexican, be more Mexican.

But no.

I looked like a pale girl with features that made people ask what my nationality was.

"Cesi. Such a strange name. And your features are interesting, too. Where did you say your parents are from? Portugal? Brazil? Spain?" they would ask.

Somehow they never thought I might be more than one thing. I might be more than one color. They certainly never thought I would come from such a lowly little country as Mexico.

Chapter 15

I stared at the giant brown brick towers in front of me. They were ugly. There were long lines of dusty cars going in between the towers in both directions. I was suddenly very glad for Tony's company. "Uh, which way do we go?"

"The pedestrians go over here, up this ramp. I always wanted to bring my roller blades here. I think it would be fun."

I understood as soon as I started to climb the winding ramp. It went around and around, but was really smooth. "Are we gonna need to do anything here . . . ?" I asked.

"Nah. The immigration officers don't care who goes into Mexico—just who comes out of it. Who would want to run away from America to Mexico unless you're a bank robber or something? Are you a bank robber?"

I laughed and gulped nervously. I walked silently beside him, lugging my bag. We were suddenly on a long walkway filled with sunlight and—children! Everywhere. Little children were calling out, "*¡Chicles! ¡Chicles!*"

There were crowds of people shoving through these kids, many no older than five. The kids were all wearing raggedy old clothes that I wouldn't have thrown in the rag bag. One kid was wearing a fluorescent pink Minnie Mouse sweatshirt, which depressed me more than anything else I had seen in my life. Something about Minnie's smiling face on the sweatshirt, which was two sizes too small for the little girl wearing it, made me remember all the times I had been to Disneyland, or wore a sweatshirt with Minnie Mouse on it. I had always thought I was so poor. My friends and I would go to the mall and walk around complaining about how poor we were. We had no idea what "poor" really meant. I understood now what Tony was talking about on the train. *Chicles* was gum.

"*¡Chicles! ¡Chicles!*" Each of these children held a worn cardboard box they had somehow fashioned into a gum-carrying case complete with cardboard handles. Most of the little cardboard boxes were patched with duct tape and were dirty at the corners. Inside the tattered boxes held by the tattered children were neat, new little packages of "Chiclet" gum. The tiny, brightly colored gum was hard, like sucking candy, when you first popped it into your mouth, and it lost its flavor in all of about thirty seconds. I must've bought it a million times from those coin-operated machines at the grocery store.

I looked around. Tony was nowhere to be found. I was alone. At some point while I watched those kids and thought about malls and grocery stores, I lost sight of Tony. I thought we were going to visit his aunt. He knew there was no way I could get out of this crowd without him. I couldn't believe he could be so selfish and leave me alone like this. I was left with these children who made me want to cry. I had to think. I had to remember what I had planned to do before I met Tony. Otherwise I was going to be stranded with the children.

Then I saw him. There was a swarm of kids around him with huge smiles on their faces and their palms outstretched. Tony had one kid attached to his swinging arm. Another was struggling to stand up under the weight of Tony's duffel bag, wearing Tony's Angel's cap. One was perched precariously on his shoulders, almost covering Tony's eyes as she clutched his hair with her small hands. All of Tony's pockets were bursting with gum. I giggled with relief and walked over to join him. He wasn't joking when he said he didn't need any gum.

Chapter 16

B ang. Bounce. Bang. Bounce. Bang! I listened to the sounds of my brother playing handball on the garage door. I didn't want to. I wanted to watch TV. But that was really a challenge when your brother was playing handball on the garage door and the garage was right next to the front door, which was right next to the TV. Aurgh!

I was about to go out and yell at him to stop it, when it occurred to me that this was the first time in a very long time that my brother had been home during the day. Weird. I jumped off the couch and pushed through the screen door to stand on the front porch.

Max was all sweaty, and when he sweat his hair got all wet too. He had taken off his shirt and his brown body was shiny in the afternoon sunlight. His face was pulled into a tight snarl and I realized that he wasn't just playing handball. He was really smashing that ball HARD! He must be pissed about something.

Max stopped suddenly and turned to glare at me, clutching the ball in his hand. "What?" he growled.

Max was fifteen going on sixteen. He was in high school and had friends who could drive. I wondered for a second if he ever thought about . . .

"What do ya want? What are you staring at?" He was not happy.

"Is everything all right?" I asked.

His snarl softened slightly. He turned back to the garage and began throwing the ball again. He mumbled, "I'm fine."

I sat down on one of the porch steps; the coolness of the cement pressed against my thighs. "Okay. You just don't seem fine, that's all. I'm sure the garage would agree with me."

He smiled a little, but didn't stop smashing the ball. "I've just got things on my mind, kid."

"Oh, yeah. I know how that is." I rested my head in my hands and looked out at the yellowing grass. The sun warmed the tips of my toes.

Max stopped again and looked at me. "Something on your mind too?"

"I dunno, Max. I feel kinda stupid saying anything, but do you ever think about Dad's side of the family? Like why no one ever talks about it or anything?"

Max wiped the sweat off his forehead with his arm and walked over to where I was sitting. "Sure I've thought about it, but I figured since no one else seemed to care, it couldn't be that important, ya know?"

"Even though it's our family?"

"Well, I guess I've always figured that whenever Dad's ready to talk, he will. That's all."

I pushed at a dead leaf with my toe. "What would you say to me having a plan . . . a way to get some information about our family?"

"Cool, I guess. What's the plan?" Max walked closer to the porch, blocking the sun, leaving my toes in the shadows.

"I don't really want to talk about it right now—but you'll know when it happens." I smiled at my brother.

"Ooh. Sounds mysterious. My sister—Cesi Holmes!" He threw me into a headlock and then laughed before he leaped up the porch steps and into the house.

I felt the sun back on my toes and wiggled them.

Chapter 17

I was still laughing at Tony when he slid the kid off his shoulders, grabbed his duffel bag, and then suddenly grabbed me. "Come on!" he yelled and took off running down the ramp. The little kids chased after us at first, but then stopped when they realized just how fast we could go.

I laughed as I ran, the backpack heavy on my back, gasping for breath. I noticed that the scenery changed again. There were little carts everywhere, overflowing with brightly painted pottery, paper flowers, marble chess sets, thick woolen blankets. My eyes couldn't take it all in fast enough as I ran past. Then I realized that Tony was leading me toward a line of yellow taxi cabs. I caught up to him, just as he finished talking to one of the taxi drivers. To my surprise, Tony slid into the taxi's back seat. "Hurry up!" he yelled.

"What are you doing? Do you really think it's safe?" I hissed at Tony, my heart pounding.

Tony pulled me into the taxi, and onto the fake leather seats, "No, it's not safe at all."

I was still hanging half out of the car. "What? Are you crazy?" I had visions of homicidal, kidnapping taxi drivers. Tony leaned across me to close the car door, "Yeah, I'm crazy, but this is the easiest way to get downtown. Besides, think of it as an experience." He smiled that crazy smile again and leaned back into the seat. I couldn't help but relax—a little.

I pulled my backpack onto my lap and tried to look as relaxed as Tony did. I reached around for a seat belt, but couldn't find one. The driver climbed into the front seat and the engine roared to life.

"Tony, I can't find the seat belts. Tony, where are they?" I whispered urgently, visions of crash test dummies on my mind.

Tony's flashing eyes glanced at me. "There aren't any." Then he closed them.

I struggled to keep myself from jumping out of the taxi as it tore out of the parking lot. I held as tightly as I could to my bag and stared at the rosary beads and blue tree air freshener swinging in broad angles from the rearview mirror. They were both hanging from the mirror. I looked at the back of our driver's head. He was singing loudly along with the Spanish music that blared out of the speaker next to my right ear. I looked out the window and saw brown hills covered with little buildings. There were bulletin boards everywhere, just like in America, except here they were all in Spanish. I was really in Mexico!

Then a bright yellow flash blocked my view of the brown city, as another taxi almost slammed into my side of the car. I squealed and looked to Tony in a panic, but his eyes remained peacefully closed, the smile still firmly on his face.

I tried to breathe deeply, looking toward the windshield. I noticed for the first time that there were no lane markings on the highway! Cars were just driving and swerving wherever they wanted to go. Out of the corner of my eye I saw a statue stuck firmly on the dashboard. It was St. Martin—Nana's saint. That had to be a good sign.

I started to feel a little better until I glanced at the steering wheel and the little dials on the dashboard. There was the speedometer all right, but it had no needle! There was no way to tell how fast we were going. I clamped my hand over my mouth to keep myself from screaming. Instead, I started to pray to St. Martin. I hoped he understood English.

Chapter 18

Mom rushed around the house, dusting, mopping, vacuuming, and talking to herself, all with Neil Diamond's latest CD blasting from the stereo. I could hear, even over all this noise, the sound of the lawn mower in the backyard. Max was mowing down the yellowed weeds, which had been growing for the past month, since the last time he mowed, which was also the last time Grandma Maryann visited.

I sat on the cold linoleum floor and scrubbed the floorboards in the kitchen. So many smells attacked my nose at once! There was the smell of bleach coming from the bucket I was dipping into. There was the smell of freshly kicked up dust coming from the vacuuming and cleaning going on in the living room, and over it all was the sour smell of old weeds and gas coming from the lawn mower. These were the smells of company coming.

I never understood why Mom went to all this trouble before Grandma came. After all, the place was all dirty and smelled like cigarettes only two hours after she arrived.

I heard a car screech on our gravel driveway, and the sound of the vacuum stopped suddenly. "Crumb!" Mom yelled from the living room. Oops, Grandma was early, and Mom wasn't done cleaning. I stayed scrubbing the floorboards, but tried to listen as Mom turned off Neil and scurried into the bathroom.

Slam. Car door. Crunch, rustle, crunch, rustle. Someone carrying something as they walked up the gravel driveway. Click, clack, click. Someone's boots climbing the front steps. Ding dong. Uh-oh!

"Cesi, could you get that please?" Mom called out in a sweet voice. Oh sure, send the girl in the ripped up shorts, with dirty water up to her armpits to greet her grandmother. I sighed, dropped the sponge into the bucket, and walked to the front door. There, standing behind the screen, was Grandma Maryann. Her sunglasses were pushed back on top of her head. She was wearing a denim shirt tucked into jeans with a turquoise and silver belt. And, of course, alligator-skin cowboy boots.

Grandma smiled. "Come on, Ces. Let the old lady in before she dies from heatstroke out here on this porch."

I unlocked the screen and fell into my grandma's hug. She smelled like rose-scented powder and cigarettes. She pulled away from me and looked me up and down. "Glad to see you dressed up for your grandmother."

I laughed as she brushed a smudge off my cheek. "I'll go get myself a glass of water while you get your mama. Tell her to hurry up. I know she's not much better off than you, Cinderella."

I didn't have to fetch Mom, because she just then came out of the hallway, clean and fresh looking, wiping her hands on her pants. "Hi, Mother! You're looking good," she said as she went to hug Grandma. "Go tell your brother to come in and clean up, Ces. And then go wash yourself up." I ran out to yell to Max as my grandma laughed about catching my mother unprepared.

Chapter 19

Apparently St. Martin did understand English, because we managed to get off the highway and onto a big, crowded street that Tony called "downtown." I jumped out of the taxi as Tony paid the man. After all, why should I pay? It was his idea to take that crazy ride. I looked around.

There were stores everywhere; crowds of people filled the sidewalks, almost all of them tourists. Almost all of them were white. Tony stood next to me and said, "Let's grab a little snack before we go to my aunt's. I don't think she's home from work yet anyway."

He didn't wait for my answer as he walked away from me. I had no choice but to follow him. I couldn't believe I was finally in Mexico. It was so different from any other place I had been. All the little carts I saw when we first crossed the border seemed to have grown up into stores here. Store after store sold rugs, ponchos, pottery, games, leather, clothes and more. The funny thing was that every store seemed to basically sell the same things, at the same prices. Weird. And there was such a difference in what the different colored people were doing. The brown people were doing all the selling. The white people were doing all the buying. Well, there were some brown people buying too—just no white people selling.

"*¡Amigos! ¡Miren! ¡Miren!*" they yelled at us as we passed. Tony's smile never faltered, and his pace never slowed. I was having a hard time keeping up with him. I wanted to shop around a little. I tugged on his arm when I saw a pair of Nikes on sale for $20.00.

"Hey, Tony, can we stop here for a second?" I asked.

"Those are fake, Cesi. You know that, don't ya?" he said without even glancing back at me.

I blushed. I was glad he wasn't looking at me. I blushed way too easily. "Uh, of course I knew that. I was just impressed by how much they looked like the real things."

"What do you expect? That's what they do for a living, make fake things look like real things," he said.

Just then, a crowd of people came tumbling out of a doorway with a loud pounding beat following them. They tripped over each other, sang, and paid no attention to where they were going. They shoved me into some more people who were coming from the other direction. All these people smelled really gross—like beer and cigarettes. Suddenly, I found myself trapped in this loud mess of people and I couldn't untangle myself.

I started to sweat. I was afraid to lose Tony. I couldn't seem to get away from these people. I felt so small. "Excuse me!" I yelled as I tried to shove my way through them. I felt shaky and sweaty. I was going to cry. I tried to take a deep breath, but there wasn't enough air. It felt like a hot, wet towel was covering my nose and mouth. I couldn't even see their faces. I only felt their sweaty, stinky bodies wrapped in T-shirts and tank tops. They were all pressing even closer. I felt a hand tightly grab my shoulder and pull.

I yelped as I was roughly tugged from the crowd. I made a fist to punch whoever was grabbing me when I realized it was Tony.

"Hey, Curious George! Keep up, I'm hungry," he said with a smile.

I was still gasping for air when Tony started trotting off again.

Chapter 20

I sat in the kitchen on the little red stool Mom bought me when I was small so I could reach the counter. Now that I was tall enough to reach most of the things in the kitchen, I hardly used it any more, except when Grandma was visiting. My grandma sat in one of the dining room chairs she dragged into the kitchen. The only room in the house she was allowed to smoke in was the kitchen. There was a vent in the ceiling that sucked up all the smoke from burnt food, and apparently burning Marlboros. We waited for Mom and Max to come back from Kentucky Fried Chicken with our dinner.

Grandma crunched on a piece of ice from her glass and stared out the window, which opened to the backyard. She said, "So kid, what's on your mind?"

"Huh?" I said.

"Oh, come on, now. I may be old, but I know when something's up with my grandkids, and your mind is not really on me right now, is it?" Her eyes never left the window, which somehow made me feel like I could talk to her more.

"I dunno. I was just thinking about my dad," I muttered.

"Oh, cause he had to work today?" she asked.

"No. It's just like . . . Well, I don't know much about him . . . I mean, about where he comes from. You know what I mean?"

"Wasn't he born in Arizona?" Grandma took a sip of her iced tea.

"I know that. It's just that he never talks about being Mexican . . ."

"Does your mom ever talk about being Irish or Cherokee?" she asked.

"No, not really, but when I ask her a question about it, she'll answer me. But Dad avoids all that stuff. I mean, he doesn't even speak Spanish in front of us," I said.

My grandmother looked down at her cigarette. "Well, maybe he doesn't know how to answer you. What kinds of things do you want to know?"

I looked at her. She was finally looking back at me. Maybe she would answer me. After all, she had known my father since he started to date my mother. "Well, what was it like when he was a kid? Did he speak Spanish? Were there other little Mexican kids where he grew up? Did he ever live in Mexico? Does he have any family that still lives there? Who were his grandparents? What did he get for Christmas? You know, stuff like that."

Grandma laughed. "Oh, is that all? You have a lot of questions there, kiddo." She put her cigarette back to her lips and took a deep breath. "Well, I can help you out with a few. I know he spoke Spanish when he was a kid. That's all his family spoke for a while. I know he had some cousins that used to live in Mexico. Then they moved to the United States. I'm pretty sure one or two moved back to Mexico a few years back. Not too long after you were born. But I never met them. That's all I know."

I sighed. I guessed it was something.

"They all sound like good questions, but why do you want to know the answers so badly?" She asked.

I watched the cigarette burning between her fingers. I didn't know how to tell her that I was looking to find out stuff about myself through my dad. It sounded too weird, even to me.

"I don't know," I lied.

Grandma snuffed out her cigarette and put her hand on my head. "Has it ever occurred to you, Cesi, that maybe your dad can't answer all your questions because his childhood was just as confusing as yours is now? Maybe even more?"

She didn't even wait for an answer. She just left the kitchen to help Mom and Max carry in dinner.

Chapter 21

"*D*os," Tony said to the teenage boy, not much taller than Tony, standing behind the corn cart. The smell of roasting corn reminded me that I hadn't eaten in a while. Maybe that was why I got so upset back there in that crowd. I hadn't really been afraid. I was just shaky from being hungry. Either way, the sweet smells coming from the cart were reminding me that this town had its positives and its negatives.

Tony handed me the corn covered in chili powder, lime, salt, and pepper. He shooed away my money, then took a big bite of his snack. Through corn-filled lips he asked, "So, where else have you been in Mexico?"

I was savoring a burnt kernel covered in lime when the question hit me. "Um, I guess I've only ever been here. Why?"

Tony started to walk more slowly as the juice from the corn dribbled down his arm. "Just some comments you made here and there about Mexico. Tijuana is really not Mexico. Know what I mean?"

I thought about it as I took another bite. "No?"

"Tijuana is all tourists, and cement, and . . . well, it's really kinda ugly. Actually most places Americans go aren't like the real Mexico."

I laughed at Tony. "Aren't you an American?"

"Hmm . . . I guess I had never thought of myself that way, but I guess I am. I just always think of Americans as tourists with a lot of money."

"Even when you're in America?" I asked.

"Nah. In America I feel even more Mexican than here, but the Americans aren't really very touristy in Fullerton." Tony licked the drizzle of juice off his arm.

"Okay, so if this isn't 'Mexico,' then what is?" I saw from the smile that was dancing on his lips that I had asked the right question.

"Mexico is green and brown. It's little villages with big farms, and lots of grass, and towns where electricity is something not everyone has. It's spicy chilis, juicy tomatoes, and light tortillas. It's music, and laughter, and pride. People just forget all that stuff. Don't ya think?"

I thought about my father and what Nana had said to him. I was beginning to think he was one of the people who had forgotten.

Chapter 22

What Grandma Maryann said made me feel worse, and yet more curious. After all, what was it about Dad that made him so quiet about his life as a kid? I hadn't really thought that his life could have possibly been more complicated than mine.

I wandered through my house that afternoon, while Mom napped to recover from grandma's visit. I felt like a detective in my own home, looking for clues. I was sneaking through the hallway when I came upon the linen closet. It had always been there, but it had never occurred to me to look inside it during my little search. It wasn't the old sheets and towels that were interesting. It was what else was in the linen closet—"the family archives."

That's what Max always called the large plastic crate on the top shelf. It was crammed with photo albums, scrapbooks, and shoebox after shoebox filled with snapshots patiently waiting to be put into their proper place in the albums.

My parents had been trying to get me to help them

put the pictures into some kind of order, and I had, but only *my* pictures. All the black and white and faded color photos of a bunch of people I really didn't know were boring to me. Until today.

I dragged my little red stepstool from the kitchen, hoping I wouldn't wake my mother in the process. Even with the stepstool, I had to stand on my tiptoes to reach the crate. I grabbed onto its plastic handles and pulled it out of the closet, almost losing my balance.

My muscles wanted to drop the heavy box, but the fear of my mother hearing a loud crash and rushing out of her bedroom to find her only daughter lying on the floor, unconscious, with precious family mementos surrounding her, was all the inspiration I needed to keep my arms strong and my feet steady. I lugged the thing into my bedroom, even though it would have been much easier to drag it, but also much noisier.

I pulled out my photo album first. The first two pages were filled with twenty snapshots of me at the hospital when I was born. I put that album aside, as well as my brother's. Mom's was next, and then my parents' wedding album. I stacked all these familiar albums, one right after the other on top of my bed. My father's album was the last. I had gone through it before. Almost all of the pictures were from college and when he first started dating my mother.

Under all of these heavy books were what I was looking for: the shoeboxes. They contained all the unorganized photos. The first box I opened was almost all family shots, with all four of us. Well, except for the oldest ones, which had Max in them but not me, because I hadn't been born yet.

We still hadn't bought an album to place all these group pictures in. There were tons of them, for every holiday and family gathering we had apparently ever been to.

I found another box with just pictures of Max. That's when I figured out that these boxes were organized by the person, or by the people in the pictures. I searched through the boxes until I recognized Dad's by the picture that was on top of the others. I knew it was Dad because we had the same picture hanging up in our hallway, except bigger. He was in high school and wearing a letterman's jacket. Although the picture was in black and white, I knew the jacket was red because Dad still had it in his closet.

There were quite a few pictures of Dad in high school. Some with him in a football uniform, others with my aunts, a couple with him standing next to a car wearing a T-shirt and jeans. One of the pictures was an exact copy of the one Grandma Maryann had in her apartment. The pictures started to get older, and Dad started to get younger the further I looked.

Finally, I ran across a bunch of pictures of Dad as a kid. He was with his two sisters standing next to a tree, or a car, or in front of a young woman, who was probably Nana. There were class pictures, too. That was when I started to notice something weird.

The class pictures were a lot like the ones my class took: a bunch of kids standing together next to their teacher, with a little sign at their feet explaining what class they were in and who their teacher was. But that's where the similarities ended.

These kids were not smiling. Neither was their teacher. And they were standing outside in front of what looked like a stone wall, instead of the auditorium curtain that I was used to. The ground beneath their feet was dirt and rocks, and there was not a tennis shoe on any kid. They were all wearing what looked like dark leather boots or shoes with laces. And the lack of smiles wasn't the only thing that was strange about the children's faces. They were mostly white. None of them were black, or Asian, and there were only a few brown faces. One of them I recognized as Dad's. All of the class pictures were like this, the kids were different ages, and the teachers were different, but there always seemed to be the same number of brown faces (three or four). The rest of the class was white.

My class was a lot more mixed up than that. There were so many different kinds of kids in our class that one of the usual lunchtime conversation topics was what nationality we were. I wondered what it must have been like for Dad as a kid in a class like that. I had no idea if he could've been happy or even if he had any friends.

I sifted past the class pictures and into the younger ones when I heard Dad call from the living room, "Hey, where *is* everybody?"

Chapter 23

"Okay, so here's a question for ya, do you want to walk another hour, or do you want to take a bus to my Aunt Delfina's house?" Tony asked as we neared the end of the long strip of stores, bars, and food carts.

"Depends. How scary is the bus?" I asked with a grin.

"Hmmm . . . doesn't go as fast as a taxi, so I would say definitely less scary, but it sure isn't Amtrak."

I felt brave. "All right, I'll give it a whirl."

Almost on cue, a dusty blue and white bus rumbled up, crammed with people. I took a deep breath and climbed on. Tony was right. It wasn't as fast as a taxi. It crawled. I was beginning to think we would have been better off walking, when it suddenly switched speeds from a crawl to a jog.

It was the kind of bus that jumped and bounced over every bump in the road, and there were a lot of bumps. I tried to hold onto a bar attached to one of the seats I was standing next to, but when we hit a really big pothole I went flying into Tony, or even more embarrassing, some other passenger who didn't even know me.

I looked around at all the faces. Mine was by far the palest. Everyone else was a shade of brown, some dark like my brother, others just a shade or two darker than me, but still tan. No one seemed to notice me standing there, falling into their shopping bags. Maybe they knew I was one of them. *I* wasn't sure if I was.

The bus came to a grinding halt. I was just about to fall over for the millionth time when Tony said, "This is us, let's get off." I followed him down the steps. We were the only two to leave the bus.

We were in a townsquare of some sort, with a big fountain in the middle. The fountain's waters were filled with kids. The area around the fountain was surrounded by dozens of other kids of all shapes and sizes, as well as a few teenagers and a couple of old people. Everyone either had their feet or their whole body deep in the water. Or else they sat close enough for the cool mist to wet their hot faces.

Tony ripped off his tennis shoes and took off his T-shirt. "Come on, Cesi, let's go cool off after that bus ride!" As usual, he didn't even wait for my answer before he jumped into the fountain's waters and disappeared in the crowd.

I walked over to the fountain and watched the children playing, laughing and splashing. The old people were smiling, and even the teenagers were smirking. It was a hot summer day and they all found a cool spot. I wanted to jump in, but that would mean I had to leave my backpack and take off my shoes, and I wasn't sure I wanted to risk losing my money that way. After all, I couldn't very well dig through my stuff, and then move all my money to my pockets.

I shifted from foot-to-foot, feeling my backpack, which had once seemed so light, get heavier. Sweat dripped off my forehead. Tony's black head popped out of the water, "Cesi! Over here!" I smiled at the sight of a kid crawling up Tony's back, giggling the whole time. Before I spent one more second thinking about it, I pulled off my shoes and bag and jumped into the fountain.

Chapter 24

I couldn't decide whether I should try to put the pictures away, or just call to Dad like I usually did when he came home. The problem with that was he usually came into whatever room I was in and right then I was surrounded by pictures. I felt guilty for looking at family photos. But there wasn't anything wrong with looking through pictures, was there? I mean, it wasn't like they were hidden somewhere and I snuck into Mom and Dad's bedroom to find them, like the Christmas presents they kept in their closet behind the shoe tree.

The pictures were stored in the linen closet where anyone in the family who was tall enough, or had a step stool, could get to them. I sighed, and then called back, "I'm in my room," and started to pack the pictures up again. I had no idea what I was afraid of. It wasn't like he was going to say, "Cesi! How dare you! Family pictures are for grownups only." But I wanted to ask him my questions without him knowing exactly how interested (obsessed) I really was. I heard him walk into the kitchen and open the fridge. There was no way I could get them all packed up by the time he got to my bedroom.

I was right. Dad knocked lightly on my door and then pushed it open enough for his head to peek in. His eyes scanned the pictures I was holding in my hands.

"Hey kid, what are you up to?"

I looked up at him and once again had to decide whether to lie or not. I decided to tell the truth.

"I was just trying to learn more about our family."

Dad pushed the door open all the way and stepped into the doorway, a smile on his face. "Really? You sure seem to be curious lately. What are you doing, starting a family tree?"

"No. I'm trying to learn more about how our family got to be the way it is now. You know, like what it was like when you were a kid, what your family was like . . ."

Dad smiled at me and came closer, "Wow, I forgot we had these pictures. I haven't looked at them in years."

"So, Dad, what *was* it like when you were a kid? What were you like?" I asked.

Dad sat at the edge of my bed, his eyes glued to the pictures. He shuffled through them, stopping to look at one or two for a few seconds longer. I thought I saw him frown before he said, "Oh, Cesi, I suppose I was a lot like you and Max. I played football, and rode my bike. I fought with my sisters. Nothing special."

"Really? What about school? What was that like?"

He flipped back to the school pictures. "I went to school until fifth grade in Arizona. I was good at it. I always got good grades."

"Was it in English or Spanish?" I asked.

"English. There was no such thing as a 'bilingual' class when I was your age. You had to learn English on your own. There was no one to teach you. So I was really quiet and listened all the time until I learned. You see, your aunts and I didn't speak English until we got to school, even though we were born in the States, because your Nana never spoke English."

I tried to imagine what it must have been like to try to learn stuff like math and history when you couldn't even understand the language your teacher was speaking. "Wasn't that hard? That doesn't seem very fair."

"Cesi, you're always going on about fair. I'm not sure if it was fair or not, but I learned English, didn't I? So it must have worked. That's what's important," he said.

"But, Dad, it looks like you were one of the only Mexican kids in the class. Wasn't that weird? Did anyone make fun of you?" I straightened up on the bed.

Dad's eyes never left the class picture he was staring at. His little fourth grade self, wearing a crisp white shirt and slacks. "No, my class wasn't like yours, Cesi, with so many different kinds of kids. But was it hard to be Mexican? I guess so. It's always hard to be different. And there weren't that many of us in school. I was lucky, though. I had a cousin who was in the same class."

"Were you ever embarrassed or anything? Did the other kids ever make fun of you?"

Dad's eyes finally met mine. "Gee, Cesi, you're just full of questions. Being a kid is tough. No matter what. You sound like Nana with all your questions. Are you sure you haven't been talking to her?" He laughed.

"Very funny, Dad. You know she wouldn't understand me."

"Well, maybe you should give her a call anyway, ask her what I was like when I was a kid. I could translate for you."

"That would be great. Maybe you could start teaching me how to speak Spanish, too, so I can talk to her more." I was excited by the prospect.

"Maybe." He answered, but by the way he said that one word, I could tell he meant no.

Chapter 25

"Oh, my God! Oh, my God!" I yelled. Really yelled. People around the fountain stared at me and I didn't care.

"Calm down, Cesi. I can't understand you when you're yelling." Tony stood beside me, dripping wet. For the first time since I met him he didn't have a smile on his face.

"I can't believe this happened. This isn't L.A. or something. Oh, my God! What am I going to do?" I whipped around and grabbed Tony by his bare wet shoulders. His eyes were concerned, and confused.

"Cesi, you are not making any sense. Why don't you sit down and tell me what happened?" I sat on the edge of the fountain, which was slowly clearing out now. The kid I was going to buy a mango from had long since disappeared.

"Tony, it's gone. My money. From all my hiding places. It's all gone!"

"Hiding places? What are you talking about? Don't you have any in your pockets?"

I reached into my soggy shorts and pulled out my $20.00. "This is all I've got, it's for the muggers."

"How thoughtful of you," he joked.

"Shut up. That's not funny. I was mugged, but they didn't take what they were supposed to!"

"Huh?" Tony's eyes looked more confused than ever.

"I went to go buy a mango. Swimming always makes me really hungry, and I went to get my money from my shoes, but it wasn't there anymore. I mean my shoes were, but my money was gone. So I went to my backpack, but it was open, and all the money was gone. All of it!" I wrapped my arms around myself to try to stop from shaking.

"Wow, Cesi. That's terrible," Tony said quietly.

I could tell he felt bad. He wanted to make me feel better, but he was only making it worse. Just looking at his kind face was making me angry. I was having a good time until someone came and ruined it all. It was all my fault too. I knew better than to just leave my stuff around some fountain in Mexico. "I can't believe I was that stupid, that I trusted these people. I should have known better." I put my head in my hands.

Tony stood up. He looked angry. "What do you mean 'these' people?"

I closed my eyes. "You know what I mean, Tony. Don't be stupid." I couldn't believe he was arguing with me at a time like this.

He yelled at me, "Who's stupid? You're the one who just forgot that you're one of 'these' people. So am I. So is your dad. Whoever stole your money was a jerk, but there are jerks everywhere. That doesn't mean all Mexicans are jerks."

". . . but, Tony . . ." I started. He didn't understand what I was saying. He was different. My dad was different. But the people who stole the money from me, well, they were the Mexicans I had always been warned about on television.

"No. I can't believe you would judge somebody based on what they look like, or what language they speak, or where they live. You, after I've helped you out as much as I have. I am proud to be one of 'these' people."

I looked up at him again. He didn't look angry anymore. He looked hurt. I felt a knot in my stomach when I realized what he said was true. "I'm sorry, Tony. I didn't mean that."

He sat down next to me again. "I know. But Cesi, jeez. I mean, there are enough white people who think we're bad and lazy and dirty without us thinking it about ourselves. We've got to be proud of who we are. Stand up for ourselves, not hate ourselves."

I looked at him. I was getting it. I just wasn't sure what I was getting yet. I had this feeling, like the feeling I got when I started to learn something. I got it when

I first studied the Knights of the Round Table, but didn't totally get the whole "chivalry" thing. Everything was starting to click. It was a good feeling, but it was also a woozy one.

I needed to do something to show Tony I trusted him, trusted *them*. "Come on, Tony. Maybe your aunt wouldn't mind having me over for dinner before I go home. I'm still hungry."

Chapter 26

Dad stood up and stretched. I put the pictures back into the shoeboxes without saying a word. He looked down at the pictures again and said, "Would you like to talk to Nana tonight? I could stay on the other line and translate for you. I'm sure she has all kinds of stories to embarrass me with."

"Yeah, that sounds great, Dad. Maybe after dinner? I'll need to write up a list of questions for her before we call. I want to be prepared." I put the top back on his shoebox of pictures.

"Sure, Lois Lane. It's kind of fun to see you so interested in something that I can help you with, rather than your usual projects. I'm going to wake up Mom. Be sure you put all this stuff back the way you found it, okay?" He raised his eyebrow when he said it and then walked into the hallway.

I rushed through putting the "family archives" back in order. I could hardly wait to pull out my journal and start my new list of questions. There were so many I wanted to ask . . . then I remembered something important—Dad was going to be the translator. Didn't that mean he could not ask a question I wanted, or not tell me the complete truth about what Nana said? Would he do that? What if there really was something he didn't want me to know, even though all I really wanted to know was about myself?

I spent the rest of the afternoon writing and re-writing questions for Nana. My journal was filled with lists and crossed-out lists.

Finally, we all sat down for dinner. I barely sat still. Max kicked me under the table twenty-seven times. I ignored him. Finally, as he passed me the rice, he said, "So how's it going, Sherlock?"

Mom raised one eyebrow and my father smiled. "Do you mean Cesi's little family history hunt, Max?"

Max's mouth was full of lettuce so he could only nod.

"It's funny you should mention that because Cesi and I are going to call Nana as soon as the dishes are done. Ces has a few questions she wants to ask. I'm sure Nana would know more about all this stuff than I do." Dad looked at me and winked.

Mom smiled, even though I could tell she was kind of surprised. "That's great, John. Cesi was talking to me the other day, and I didn't even know where to begin. Max and I can work on the dishes so you two can get right to it."

Max burst out, "But, Mom, tonight's Cesi's dish night . . ."

"Oh, Max, one night won't kill you. Besides this is a family project. I'm sure it will be fun for all of us to find out what Cesi discovers."

Max kicked me again under the table. This time harder. But I was too excited to let it bother me.

🌞 🌞

"Hello, Nana?" I yelled into the phone. Although Nana was only in San Diego, and the connection was good, her hearing wasn't that great.

"Cecilia?" she answered back.

"Hi, Mom," Dad added.

After hearing his voice, Nana broke off into Spanish with Dad only interrupting with a few "uh-huh's" whenever she stopped to take a breath.

Finally, Dad said, "Go ahead, Cesi. She's ready."

I sat down on the cold kitchen floor. I had a feeling this was going to be a long conversation. Dad sat in the living room on the other phone. It was weird to hear his voice in one ear from the living room and in the other ear from the phone. I took a breath and then asked, "Where did Dad and his sisters and you and grandpa live when he was young? What was it like?"

There was a deep breath taken in San Diego, and then Nana started to reply in rapid Spanish. When she stopped speaking, Dad began to translate, "She was born in Nogales. It's a town that stretched across the Mexican and U.S. border. That was where she met Dad and where all of us kids were born. When we were old enough to start school, Dad got a new job and we moved into a town in Arizona. We went to school there until I was in fifth grade—then we moved to California. Arizona is the desert, so it's hot during the day and cold at night. We lived in a small town, in a little tiny house. All three kids shared one room, and Mom and Dad shared the other room. I guess that's it."

"What was Dad like when he was a kid?" I asked.

I heard Mom laugh at that question as she dried the dishes. "Perfect, I'll bet, " she said quietly.

Nana's voice took on a happy sound, almost like she was smiling, even though I could barely understand a word she was saying other than the occasional *m'ijo*.

Once again Dad's voice came back on the line and he said, "She said I was the most wonderful child a woman could ever want. I would have to agree with her."

I laughed and then asked, "What was he like in school? What kind of grades did he get?"

My father asked the question in Spanish, and Nana answered again, but this time, while her voice started out happy, it changed, and Dad said something back to her in Spanish. They had started a different conversation, and they went on like that for a few minutes. It almost seemed like they were arguing about something. Finally, I cut in, "Dad, what are you guys saying?"

He cleared his throat and said, "Nana said I was a good student. I always got good grades, but I stopped speaking Spanish so much at home and started only speaking English to my sisters. She thinks I was trying to pretend I wasn't Mexican. It wasn't that though, Cesi. I was just trying to practice my English. It was really important for me to know it, for my family to know it. So I practiced."

"Oh," I answered. I took a deep breath and then looked back at my list of questions. I realized suddenly that despite all my careful planning, I still didn't have the questions I really wanted to ask Nana written down. As a matter of fact, I really didn't know what I wanted to ask. I asked a couple more questions, but it seemed like the fun we had was now a little strained by the school argument.

I tried to end the interview as quickly as I could. Then I said good-bye to Nana, leaving my father to finish up the conversation, and Max and Mom to finish the dishes. I needed to get some air. I pushed open the front screen door and went out to the porch.

Chapter 27

Aunt Delfina's house reminded me a little of Nana's house. It was small, one-story, and filled with plants. Except it wasn't red. It was pink. Pepto-Bismol pink. Instead of music or Spanish soap operas, I only heard birds chattering and chirping as we walked up to the front door.

Tony had just reached for the doorbell when a large woman appeared at the door. She had a flowered scarf on her head and was wearing a flowered housecoat to match. When she opened the screen door I saw she had pink slippers on, which matched the house.

"*¡Ay! ¡Antonio!*" she yelled when she saw Tony. He soon disappeared into her embrace. I stood staring at her flowered head buried in Tony's hair. Then she looked up and spotted me.

"Hello. Who's your little friend, Toño?" Aunt Delfina asked.

"Oh, sorry, Tía. This is Cesi Álvarez. I met her on the train, and invited her for dinner."

Aunt Delfina looked a little confused. "Your daddy isn't John Álvarez is he?"

"Yeah. He is." It was impossible that this flowery woman with the Pepto-Bismol house would know my dad! Things like that didn't happen in real life.

Instantly, I was in her arms, too. "Oh, I haven't seen you since you were in diapers. I can't believe it! What are the chances? That's why I believe in miracles, Toño. This is why. Little miracles like this happen every day." She backed up and looked me over. "So how is your papá?"

"He's fine . . . but how do you know him?"

Aunt Delfina opened her mouth to answer, but Tony broke in. "Let's go inside and talk about this, okay, Tía?"

"Oh, I'm so sorry. I was so shocked to see her here that I forgot all about being a good host. Come in. Please."

We followed her into the house. In even more ways it reminded me of Nana's house. Lots of pictures and statues everywhere. But there wasn't a speck of dust. The place was absolutely immaculate. Tony and I sat on the couch as Aunt Delfina disappeared into the other room, which by the sounds coming from it I guessed was the kitchen.

Tony stretched out on the couch, obviously quite at home here. I looked around from my spot. Then I saw in a corner a little altar just like Nana's, except there were different people in the pictures, and the statue in the center wasn't St. Martin. It was a woman wearing pink and blue. But just like Nana's altar, there were candles, and photographs, and little objects next to the pictures. When I looked closer, one of the photographs looked familiar.

Aunt Delfina came back into the living room with three glass bottles of Coke and a bowl of peanuts, still in the shell. She smiled, but her smile caught where I was looking and got even bigger.

"Oh, so you like my *ofrenda*?" she grinned.

"Pardon me?" I asked.

"Do you know what that is, Cesi? You look confused," Tony said.

"Nana has one, but I don't know what it is," I replied honestly.

Aunt Delfina walked over to it and pointed things out as she talked. "This is my sister, and my little daughter. They both died too young. And this is my mamá." She made the sign of the cross over her chest. "And this is the Virgin of Guadalupe. She's my patron saint. I pray to her for all the people that I have loved who have gone on to Heaven before me." She stared lovingly at the pictures.

"But what are those things next to the pictures?" I asked.

"Oh. These are just some of their favorite things. In case they decide to visit me." Aunt Delfina continued to smile at the pictures.

I looked at Tony. She couldn't really think they would come visit her. But Tony had gone back to cracking peanuts. Apparently he didn't think this was strange at all.

"My Nana has something like that at her house. Except the pictures are different, and the stuff next to them is too." I continued to check out her *ofrenda*.

Aunt Delfina didn't look surprised. "Of course she does. The people she knew were different, and they liked different things. Anybody who has seen a few people pass before them has one. At least us Mexican families do."

I moved closer to the picture of a young woman. "Did you say she was your mom? She looks familiar. I think Nana has a picture just like that," I said, a little confused.

Aunt Delfina nodded. "That's my cousin Lydia. She was your Nana's brother's wife, so your Nana could have a picture of her on her *ofrenda*."

I looked up, shocked. I took a deep breath. "Does that mean we're related?" This whole impossible situation was getting weirder by the second.

Aunt Delfina smiled at the picture, not noticing the looks of surprise on my face and Tony's. "Yes, we're related, cousins I guess. That's why it's a little strange that you would just run into each other on the train. Small world, huh?"

Aunt Delfina turned back to us and then sat in a wicker rocking chair with her Coke. "So how's your daddy? I haven't talked to him in awhile."

I took a sip from my bottle. I guessed if Aunt Delfina thought it was normal to just run into your cousin on a train to Mexico, I should just let it go. I answered her, "He's fine. Were you very close to him?"

Delfina nodded. "I grew up with your daddy. We were in the same class until he moved. I guess right after the fifth grade. There weren't many kids like us in that class, so we all kind of stuck together. Then later on, when it got harder to find work in Arizona, I moved out to California for a little while and worked with him. That was before I moved here."

"So you guys were friends?" I asked.

"I guess so. Although, we were family first. In those days everyone who was related lived close to each other. People had big families. We looked after each other, but we didn't play together. Your daddy was a great football player when we were small, so he was always playing, but us girls weren't allowed to play sports. I usually just sat by myself and watched." Aunt Delfina took a sip of her own Coke and stared at one of her brightly painted walls. But it wasn't so much like she was staring at the wall as *through* it, as if she were looking out at that schoolyard of long ago.

"School was okay. It was tough though. The other kids were all white. They were always polite, but it was hard to become friends with any of them. The teachers though—well that just depended on your luck," Aunt Delfina said.

"What do you mean?" I asked.

Aunt Delfina leaned forward in the rocker and looked at us. "To begin with, we weren't allowed to speak Spanish . . ."

I interrupted, "Dad said something about that. But if you didn't speak English, then how could you . . ."

"Ah, so you see how it was hard. You had to be quiet until you were pretty sure you knew what to say in English. Otherwise . . . WHACK!" She slammed her hand down on the arm of the rocking chair.

Tony stopped cracking his peanuts for a second, "You mean they hit you if you said a word in Spanish?"

Aunt Delfina nodded. "With a ruler. Right on your knuckles. I don't have to tell you that I hardly ever talked in school. I remember one day your dad really had to use the bathroom. We must have been in second grade. He didn't know what to do until finally he just asked in Span-

ish anyway. The class laughed and then . . . WHACK!"
Aunt Delfina closed her eyes for a minute.

"Did the teacher let him go to the bathroom?" I
asked, wincing at the idea of my poor young dad getting
hit with a ruler.

"No. Of course not. He couldn't remember what to
say. So he just went back to his seat with a sore hand,
and he still had to go. He didn't even cry. He just waited until the recess bell and then ran as fast as I had ever
seen any child run, all the way to the bathroom."

"Aw, man, that's terrible!" Tony shook his head.

"Yes. It was. But we all went through it," Aunt Delfina said, quietly.

"But why didn't you tell your parents? They would
have done something," I said. Mom would have been at
the school so fast the principal's head would have spun.

Aunt Delfina shook her head. "Our parents would-
n't know what to do. They spoke even less English than
us, and because of how poor most of us Mexicans were,
we were ashamed of how our parents looked, how they
dressed. Our parents were just grateful that we got to go
to school at all. Most of them hadn't gone past the third
grade. They did their best by making sure we were as
neat and clean as possible. Our clothes were always
ironed, our hair always wet down and combed neatly.

That was how they tried to protect us." Aunt Delfina took another deep breath.

"So we had to think of ways to protect ourselves. We would practice speaking English to each other when we walked back to our own neighborhood after school. We would correct each other and compliment each other. But that wasn't really the worst thing though. The language, I mean," she said.

I wasn't sure I wanted to hear any more stories. A slap on the hand with a ruler for speaking a different language would have been enough to convince *me* not to teach my own children Spanish when I grew up. I sighed, and then looked back at Aunt Delfina.

She looked like she had just remembered something. "I haven't thought about this day in years. It was right before your daddy moved to California, so we must have been in fifth grade. People just didn't trust us. They thought we were dirty, or liars, just because we were born brown, and they were white. It didn't matter how clean our mamás scrubbed us, or what our papás taught us."

I thought of the two girls in my class last year with the too-tight braids and burrito lunches, and felt a little sick to my stomach for not even trying to be nice to them.

Aunt Delfina continued, "I had learned by that time that it was best not to stand out too much. I just did my work and never raised my hand in class. I did my best to disappear."

Tony hadn't touched the peanuts in a while. He leaned forward with me, the same look of worry on his face.

"Your daddy wasn't like me though. He was smart. He liked to talk in class. He had learned English, even though he still had an accent, and he was going to use it. Anyway, he always got straight A's, and most of the kids really liked him. He was the pride of the family. All of that didn't change the fact that he was Mexican though."

"What do you mean?" I asked in a whisper.

"Well, one day we were about to take a spelling test when Cindy Bradshaw realized her brand new set of colored pencils was missing. Now, why she thought to check them right before a spelling test, I'll never know. Anyway, our teacher Mrs. Grady called all the class to attention and asked if anyone had seen the pencils. No one had. So Mrs. Grady asked Cindy where she last had them. Cindy said she put them in the closet that very morning. So Bobby Macintosh said that whoever was last in the closet probably took them. Mrs. Grady asked who it was, even though we all knew who it was."

"Why did you all know?" Tony asked.

"Because Cesi's daddy was the closet monitor. Every morning he was the last one out of the closet, and every morning he closed them. So right in front of the entire class, Mrs. Grady asked John to come to the front of the classroom. He did. She asked him if he had taken Cindy's pencils. He said no. So calmly, he looked her right in the eyes and said no."

Aunt Delfina shook her head at the memory of it. "Well, Mrs. Grady would have none of that. She called him a filthy thief. She said he was just proof that no matter what you tried to do, you couldn't get a Mexican to change his true nature. They would always be lying, dirty and lazy. Your daddy's eyes never left hers. He didn't cry. He didn't yell. His face remained completely calm."

"So then she took the ruler out?" Tony asked quietly, not wanting to know, but unable to keep from asking.

Aunt Delfina shook her head. "No. That would have been too easy. We were all used to that. Mrs. Grady had a point to prove. Your daddy had been driving her crazy all year with his perfect grades and perfect behavior. She wanted to prove that she was right. She wanted everyone to know that she had always been right."

I was angry. "About what? What was she always right about?"

"Don't get so upset. People still feel the way she did. A lot more people in that town felt like she did than didn't. They didn't trust Mexicans for all kinds of reasons. They thought Mexicans were taking all the jobs away from the citizens, even though most of those jobs were as fruit pickers or housecleaners. Jobs most self-respecting white people wouldn't take."

I was so confused. Here Aunt Delfina was telling me this horrible story about the white people in the town my father and she had grown up in, and I was so angry at them. But at the same time, I was part white too.

As if she could read my mind Aunt Delfina said, "Not all white people were like Mrs. Grady. She just had a very popular opinion. Anyway, after Mrs. Grady had gone on for a while about how she had known all along what kind of boy John was, she had him go and make a sign to wear around his neck for the rest of the day. It said, 'Thief.' Then she tied it around his neck and had him stand at the front of the classroom wearing it with both his arms raised at his sides, as high as his shoulders. He stood that way until lunch. With his arms out like that. It must have been at least two hours. And his arms never shook. He didn't cry. His face was as calm as if he'd been lying on the beach."

"Did they ever find out who really stole the pencils?" I asked, hoping maybe there would be some justice at the end of this story.

Aunt Delfina nodded. "Funny thing was, Cesi, they were never stolen. Cindy found them in her book bag at the end of the day. She told Mrs. Grady. Mrs. Grady just nodded her head and then dismissed us."

Tony's mouth gaped open. "You mean she didn't apologize for what she did?"

Aunt Delfina smiled weakly. "No. She never did. She didn't have to."

We all sat there in silence. Waiting for something. Maybe some sort of happy ending.

Chapter 28

So there I sat, once again on the front porch. This time Max wasn't pounding away with a handball on the garage door. Dad was finishing the phone call to Nana, Mom and Max were drying the dishes. I was thinking. Thinking about all the conversations I had had in the past few days, all the questions I still had.

I felt the summer night breeze on my bare legs and the cold cement under my feet. I took a deep breath and leaned back on my elbows. I wanted to know so much and yet the question was pretty simple. Why was my father, or rather Mexico and my father, so important to me? Somehow I figured I would learn something about this person I was becoming. But I just wasn't sure what I thought I would learn. I hadn't learned what I wanted to from either books or my family. I just couldn't think of the right questions to ask. I had to go out there and try to figure this stuff out. Somehow, my dad, Mexico and I all had a lot in common, or at least had worked together to make me into the person I was today. I had to go. Otherwise, I would probably never know because

I would get too busy with my life, and maybe forget about all those people on Nana's altar. I didn't want to do that.

So the votes were in. I was going to Mexico. I would go to Tijuana since it was the only part of Mexico I could get to by train within a couple of hours. I knew my family was from Nogales, but Mexico was Mexico—right? I was going to go by myself. I was going to have to lie in order to do it because my parents would never let me go by myself. I knew I had to go alone. Funny. I was going to have to lie in order to learn the truth.

Chapter 29

The silence ended when Aunt Delfina said, "So your Nana moved her family to California. Finding jobs was supposed to be easier there. And John was excited. He thought he might fit in better. Our families stayed in touch. Your papá would tell me all sort of things about California. I eventually moved there myself. He was right; it was easier to fit in. There were more Mexicans there."

"Why didn't you stay there?" I asked.

"Even though there were a lot of Mexicans, we were still very different from the white people. There were still a lot of people who didn't want us to be taking their jobs, going to the places they liked to go . . . there still are people like that, from what I hear. Anyway, one of my aunts," she pointed to the *ofrenda*, "passed on and left this house to me, so I came here. Since I've been here, I've been pretty happy. I like it here, away from the city, but close enough, you know?"

Tony and I nodded in unison. Then I took a deep breath and leaned back on the couch again. I understood a lot more about my father and about myself than I had ever thought I would.

"But enough of all this talk about John. Where is he? Is he going to come pick you up?"

"Uh, he's at home. He's not going to pick me up. I'm taking the train home," I answered.

Aunt Delfina smiled. "Ah, *m'ija*. No, let me call him. He might not know how dangerous it is for a child to travel alone at night in this city. Besides, I would love to see him." She started towards the kitchen.

"No. Really, please . . ."

But it was too late. I heard her dialing the phone. I looked to Tony for help, but he was completely absorbed in the peanuts again.

Chapter 30

We all ate silently around the lace-covered, round dinner table in Aunt Delfina's small dining room. In the center of the table was a plate with my three lowly avocados smashed into guacamole. None of us touched it. Bird cages surrounded us. The only sounds in the room besides forks hitting plates were the birds chirping and jumping from perch-to-perch, feathers fluttering.

Aunt Delfina's jaw was tight, and Tony, my new cousin, looked embarrassed. I could barely lift my fork to my mouth. My dad was on his way.

Aunt Delfina had called Dad. My parents were sick with worry. Apparently, Mom decided to stop by Kathi's to drop off more avocados, only to discover I was never there. Kathi hadn't even known I was supposed to come over. Mom called the cops, and they searched the neighborhood. Someone at the train station remembered me, so they knew I had been to San Diego, but after that my trail disappeared. Dad was in San Diego searching the streets with the cops when Aunt Delfina called. He was on his way now.

Tony slipped his address and phone number into my hand when Delfina wasn't looking. "I'm really glad we met, and I want to stay friends, especially now that we're related and all. Something tells me we're not gonna have much time to exchange addresses once your dad gets here. I know you could probably get it from your dad, but . . . just in case."

That was the last thing he said before he clammed up. Aunt Delfina wasn't saying much after she made the initial announcement about the situation. She looked absolutely disappointed in me. Betrayed.

And I had just met her. She had told me more about myself in a few short hours than I had learned from all the time I spent searching.

I knew Dad was going to kill me. So I was forcing myself to eat, knowing this would be my last meal.

We heard a car pull up, and then I heard my father's voice talking to another man. Aunt Delfina silently got up. When she returned, my father was standing with her, his eyes red and filled with hurt.

Without looking at Aunt Delfina he said to her, "Thank you, Delfina. I have no idea how to repay you."

"No. No. I'm just glad I was the one who found her. I wish we could have met in happier circumstances. She could stay here if you would like. Maybe she needs a little time away from home? Maybe she's having some problems?"

My father's eyes never left my face. I felt like I was on fire. "No, Delfina. That's what I don't get. Everything was fine at home. She seemed so happy. She never said otherwise." He sighed. "Let's go, Cesi. We have already taken too much of Delfina's time."

I'm not sure what happened next. I must have left that house somehow. Said good-bye to Tony. Thanked Aunt Delfina. Then, I was in the back seat of a police car, and we were headed back over the border.

Chapter 31

I looked out of the car window into the Mexican darkness. We were driving over the same highway that I rode on this morning with that crazy taxi driver. This time, no taxi was even near us. I guessed the San Diego police car intimidated them.

There was a long line of cars forming at the border. There were all kinds of vans and trucks pulled over, and people in uniforms with flashlights searching through the cars. They were searching for illegal immigrants, people from Mexico trying to sneak into the United States. We didn't have to stop. We were in a police car. I caught a glimpse of some of the faces of the drivers standing outside their cars, digging into their wallets for their driver's licenses, while officers searched their cars. No one was happy.

Tony was right. They only cared if you were trying to get out of Mexico, not if you were going in.

My dad was having some sort of conversation with the cops about immigrants. I tried not to listen. His voice was tired, but I was tired too. All I wanted was to crawl into bed and sleep.

The police car pulled into a parking lot. We jumped out of the car. I walked over to Dad's car as he shook hands with the cops. I wasn't sure what I was going to say to him. I didn't know if I even wanted to say anything to him.

Chapter 32

Dad drove quietly, listening to the radio playing softly in the background. Music was playing and the words were in English. We were back on the highway. I looked up at the yellow border crossing sign. The little family in black silhouette, mom, dad, and kid—running. The sign warned drivers that people might be running across the highway trying to get into the United States. They were posted alongside the road with the speed limit signs.

Dad broke the silence. "I'm not mad at you, Cesi."

"Oh." I sighed. I didn't know what else to say.

"I think I know why you did this. I've been thinking about it. Some stuff you said to Mom, me, even Max." His eyes moved over to me for a second before going back to the road.

"What did I say?" I asked.

"You were wondering about me. About why I don't speak Spanish. About why Nana gets mad at me sometimes. Am I right?"

"Yeah." I squirmed in my seat.

"But what I don't get is why you were so interested in *my* life." He waited for me to answer.

"I don't know. It sounds stupid now, I guess. I thought that by learning about you and about Mexico, I would learn something about me. I already know all about Mom and her side of the family . . ."

He took a deep breath. "That doesn't sound stupid, Cesi. That sounds really smart. I just wish I had said something earlier, about who I am, why I do what I do. I wish you had asked."

"But I did ask. I asked Mom, Max, Grandma Maryann, you, even Nana. The problem was, I didn't know what to ask. I didn't really know what I was look-ing for." I was frustrated I even had to explain all of this to him.

"So you thought you'd find it in Mexico? In Tijua-na, no less? Tijuana is a dangerous place for a kid to be in alone. Why didn't you tell me you wanted to go? I would have taken you." His eyes glanced toward me.

"I didn't know that." I sat quietly. I looked up at the highway signs whizzing past us and kept quiet. I kept thinking about what he said. He would have answered my questions. He would have taken me where I wanted to go. But I didn't know how I could have figured that out on my own. We drove in silence for about an hour before I realized that we were not headed towards our house.

"Dad, where are we going?"

"To a place I'm sure Delfina told you all about. It's about eight hours from here, so you might as well put your seat back and go to sleep until we get there." His eyes were focused on the black road in front of us.

"What about Mom? What did she say? Does she know?" I asked nervously.

"Yeah, she's the one who suggested it. Now try to get some sleep."

I pushed my seat back. The cold air from the air conditioner, the seat belt and the thoughts whirling in my head made it difficult for me to sleep, but before I knew it, my eyes closed.

Chapter 33

When I opened my eyes again there was an orange glow in the sky as the sun began to rise over the horizon. Dad was sipping on an extra large cup of coffee. His eyes never left the road as he said, "Good morning, Cesi. You woke up just in time. Nogales is just up ahead."

I pulled my seat back up and looked at the green sign posted to my right. I read it aloud, "You are now entering Nogales."

"Yep, this was where I was born," he said. We drove into the town. It didn't look like anything special. Just small. A few trees here and there.

We drove past a row of newly built houses. "Where those houses are now was where my family first lived."

The town was just waking up, so there was only a Wonder Bread truck sharing the road with us. The town seemed so sweet in the soft sunrise light.

"Are we going to stop here?" I asked.

"No. I just thought we would drive through on our way to Douglas. The stories that Delfina told you took place there." He smiled at me and then turned back to the road.

"How do you know Delfina told me anything?"

"She's my cousin, remember? I know her pretty well. And I also know she's been keeping those stories to herself for a long time."

We rode in silence for a while longer. Slowly, other cars started to join us on the road. The silence was now punctuated by driving noises.

Finally, we reached the town of Douglas. It didn't look much different from Nogales except it had a few more trees. Pine trees. It was quiet. Not many people out this early on a Sunday morning. We drove down a quiet street and pulled into a parking lot next to a small elementary school. It didn't look too different from the school I graduated from. It was painted an ugly beige color except for the brown classroom doors.

"Looks like they built a new school," Dad said after he had turned off the engine. He opened the car door and got out, stretching as he did so.

I followed his lead, reaching my arms up and yawning, my eyes burning from exhaustion. I took a deep breath and noticed that the air smelled really clean, and crisp. It was different than the air in California. I walked over to stand next to my father. "So I guess Mrs. Grady doesn't teach here anymore, huh?"

He looked at me, not at all surprised that I knew the

terrible woman's name. "No. She died quite some time ago, I suspect. She wasn't that young when I had her."

We stood there. I didn't know what I was expecting to happen. What I expected to see. Maybe something dark and miserable looking. But this wasn't it. "Come on. Let's see the rest of the town," he said, and we jumped back into the car.

We drove up and down streets, Dad pointing out various places he had gone to, or where things used to be when he was a kid. Finally, he turned up a side road into a little wooded area. I followed him out of the car, to a dirt path lined with stones. We walked along the path until we reached what I recognized as a cemetery. There were gravestones standing amongst the trees. Dad grabbed my hand and I walked with him through the sunlight that trickled through the pine branches.

He stopped at a smooth gray tombstone. I looked down and saw the name, Adolfo Álvarez, my grandfather. I knew he died when Dad was young, but I couldn't figure out why I was standing there right now.

Dad let go of my hand and bent down to brush loose pine needles off the stone. "He moved here from Mexico City to find a better life. He couldn't find work down there, so he came here. He dressed really well. Always wore a suit. But he wasn't really an American. At least not to most of the businessmen here. He moved to Nogales, because there were a lot more Latino people there. That's where he met Mom, but he brought us all back here as soon as he could. He did all right for himself. But Douglas wasn't a good fit for me, anymore than Mexico was for him."

I finally figured out who that man in the suit was, the one whose picture sat on Nana's *ofrenda*. The one who looked like Dad.

I looked down at the stone and then back at Dad. "So you came to California looking to get away from the kinds of things that happened to you here?"

"Well, my mom was the one who moved us. I think she knew we weren't happy here. We did our best in California to fit in a little bit better than we did here. But I guess while we were busy doing that, we lost some of the important stuff along the way." When Dad looked back at me, his eyes were wet with tears.

I didn't know what to say. I had never really seen my father cry before. I certainly didn't want to be the one making him do it. "Why are you crying, Dad?" I whispered.

"Because I just realized that by trying to keep you from having the same kind of childhood I had, I made yours harder. I kept a lot of stuff from you that could have helped you."

I had nothing to say so I hugged him, burying my face in his chest, feeling his shirt buttons pressing against my cheek.

He stroked my hair and said, "I'm sorry."

We stood there for a while. I thought about how it was with our family. It seemed that the Álvarezes were a restless bunch. We always roamed. We looked for answers, and tried to change our lives in order to find them when there really weren't any answers—at least not the kind you could write down somewhere on a test.

We walked away from the grave and back to the car. The cars on the road roared past us, and more people walked up the path to visit the cemetery. The world was alive with sound. We got back into the car and started to drive west again.

We drove for hours. We stopped once to call Mom and Max and to take a quick nap. I suggested that we stop at a hotel, since Dad hadn't slept the night before. All that driving must have been exhausting for him, but he said he was in a hurry to get home.

I looked out into the dark hills that whizzed by the car. The moon was high and bright in the dark sky. I cleared my throat and said, "Dad, I learned a lot on this trip. Even if it wasn't the smartest thing in the world for me to do."

I looked over at his face now, bright in the moon-light. "I learned about Mexico. The green and brown, and corn, and laughter, and music and . . . other stuff. The good stuff. I also understand now why you felt it was a good idea to keep some things from us. I don't know if it *was* a good idea, but I can see why."

"I'm glad," he said.

"I want to share it with Mom and Max when we get home. The good and the not so good stuff. Is that okay?"

"Of course it is. We'll do it together."

I took another breath and said, "Think maybe you could teach us Spanish, too?"

He laughed, "It seems really silly now that I never did to begin with. It would be fun."

I smiled. He smiled. He was proud. I was, too. I knew who I was. The good and the bad. Just like everyone else—good and bad.

So was he. He wasn't perfect. I knew I wasn't. I screwed up royally by running away. But then again, I needed to find some things out. In the same way he thought he shouldn't tell me.

As we pulled up to our little house, safely back in California, with Mom and Max waiting for us on the front steps, I knew I had more than one home now. I always had. I just hadn't known it.

A Note About
Border Crossing

The summer before I became a teacher I took a class
on how to teach writing to children. During the class,
we talked about how important it is for children to see
people like themselves in the books they read. I thought
about what it was like when I was growing up. I never
read a book where the main character was like me. I
was short. My family did not have much money. I was
half Mexican and half Irish/Cherokee. I read a lot so I
knew if there had been a book with people like me in it,
I would have found it.

I thought about how many books had been written
since I was a kid. There were a lot more books and
those books had lots of different kinds of people, people of different shapes, religions, abilities and races. I
was happy about that. But, I still had not seen a book
with somebody like me in it.

I knew that kids like me, with mixed heritages
would probably love to read a book where the main
character dealt with some of the same problems or

questions they had. I also knew that kids who did not come from mixed heritages might want to read a book about someone different, just like I loved reading books about people who were different from me. I wished there was a book like that so that I could share it with my students. Then a little voice inside my head asked, "Why don't you write it?"

So I did.

Acknowledgments

First of all, and most importantly, I want to thank my 4th grade students past and present from P.S. 321. You helped me through drafts of the book in all its stages, made helpful suggestions and listened patiently as I talked on and on about it. (I told you I would mention you.)

I also want to thank the rest of the P.S. 321 community (teachers, staff, families and administration) for their moral support and cheerleading.

Thank you to my friends who read and re-read and made suggestions. I need to especially thank Joslyn Aubin and Tina Encarnacion for helping me retype the entire manuscript in one night when my disk was erased.

Thank you to my three best school writing teachers: Ms. Wuerer (7th Grade), Mr. Kopacki (High School) and Perry Glasser (College).

Thank you to my two writing workshops, past and present for the countless patient hours of work. Thanks particularly to Jennifer Belle for being such an influential writing teacher in my adult life.

Thank you to the Teachers College Reading and Writing Project. I got my earliest ideas for Cesi while at my first summer institute several years ago.

Thank you to my family for answering my questions while saving theirs until I was done with the book.

And thank you to Nadine for walking with me in a torrential down pour at 3:00am to a 24-hour copy shop in Times Square. Good times.